I am Ag acters,
places ar author's
imagination.
Any resemblance to actual persons, living or dead, or
actual events is purely coincidental.

Copyright © 2021 by Jackie Sansom
Mabel & Stanley Publishing
All rights reserved.

This book or any portion thereof may not be reproduced or used in any manner whatsoever without the express written permission of the publisher except for the use of brief quotations in a book review.

For Finn

I am Agnes

"Anyone who has common sense will remember that the bewilderments of the eyes are of two kinds, and arise from two causes, either from coming out of the light, or from going in to the light."

Plato

Chapter 1

Light switch

Darling Agnes

I watched you today as you sat in the dark place. Did you realise you glow? Very brightly indeed. Like the sun in a bubble. We are all in absolute awe of you. What's that 'Why isn't everyone else sunny and bubbly?' They aren't quite cooked yet my lovely sparkly one. They aren't ready to see. You… on the contrary… are ready to burst. So don't dilly dally dawdle. All you have to do is go to the door now Agnes. Just that.

Oh yes …… you might ask, 'What if I don't love it, when I go through the door, will I be able to come back?' Well, my dearest, I have never seen anyone go back. Nobody. Nope. Because there is so much here in the light that immediately you step into it, you know that you belong, woopdedoodaa! Your first lesson here is trust. Trust that once you make the step, take the step, jump, leap, cha-cha-cha and feel that sparkly warmth………. There is not an ounce of you that will want to return to the dark.

The door is yours.

I'm here, I'm there, I'm everywhere.

My love always.

Bob

Chapter 2

Shadows

I never imagined being back home at the age of 30. Back with Mum in sunny Purbrey. Nothing had changed really. One minute she was checking on me all the time, the next completely ignoring me and uttering discontented and pointed comments about my inability to cope.

My marriage to Dan had failed after one whole year. We never discussed this, but my inconsistent mood and unhealthy coping methods were a point of discussion which she greedily reiterated to her friends over the phone. I cried..... she called her friend to tell her I was crying. I got divorced, she called her friend to tell her how I had failed to keep the best man for me. I moved back home because, quite frankly, I used a bottle of vodka as a comforter. Couldn't work. Couldn't go out. Couldn't make conversation properly to be honest. So, she called her friend to tell her I was living back at home at the age of thirty. She layered the number '30' with gold and silver sparkles like it meant that I would be outcast and left to shrivel, now I was thirty. I believed it. Dad had passed away before I remember him, so she had spent her life very much alone. But somehow, this was okay ...for her.

As the days passed, I was not completely sure reaching the age of thirty-one was something I was going to greet. Being at home was easier than living elsewhere and being on my own, though I quickly realised that her huffing and puffing was not a symptom of a poor respiratory condition.

She had her routine, and I had mine. She got in, watched TV, made tea, watched the news, washed dishes, watched TV, went to bed. I did this with her sometimes. We didn't talk. Just watched the endless soap operas and dramas which seemed to affirm that life was quite sad and full of negative occurrences. Yes, there were some good bits, but they were followed by the inevitable torment of a death or failed relationship. I could feel her gaze whenever this storyline came up. 'It happens all the time... you're best off on your own,' she offered. As though she was the guru on my ability to have or to not have relationships.

But I sensed that she liked being home alone. That I was perhaps an annoyance. She came up with lots of ideas for things to do. The library, the job centre, the café, the local shops. Anywhere I could look for a job - that I wasn't capable of holding down, of course.

We never talked much about the divorce and I didn't want to. 'Only you could make a marriage last just one year, Agnes,' was her favourite. I couldn't answer this. I didn't have the ability and I suppose I did believe it was totally my fault. Dan was lovely. Dan was a kind man. Dan was the best thing to happen to me. It was just me that was the problem. Quite frankly I would rather not be here. But equally there was no other place I wanted to be. Which left me here. A space of my own in a single bedroom. And the community of my mother.

Mum worked as a cleaner at a local school, just part-time but enough to keep her busy. I can imagine her day being filled with consistent chatter to whoever she could find and whether they liked it or not. And this would now largely be about my return because she didn't have much else to talk about.

I kept myself busy and captive indoors – except for visits to the corner shop. I would go back to bed after she had left for work and in the beginning be up and dressed by the time she returned. As days went by, I felt less like getting up and so stocked up well on bottles of Russian – the cheapest I could find, and so, able to afford more.

Being alone in my room had been a catalyst for conversations with myself. From, ‘Yes, best off without them Agnes,’ and, ‘You can’t seem to keep one anyway.’ To singing and dancing to happy tunes enhanced by my favourite tipple and then to the desperateness of those lost love songs in wailing tones – again with the aid of my closest ally.

Most of all I sat on the windowsill staring out of the window, watching the people who could get on with their lives.... actually *get* on with their lives. Whilst I played with feathers popping out of my pillow.

Chapter 3

Shadows of the past

Agnes, please clean the dishes and then go for a walk. Mum.

My to do list. I had ignored all suggestions to go out for anything other than my Russian this far. Somehow today didn't seem any different bar the lack of an 'x' on Mum's note. It gave me incentive.

My desire to dress properly was limited so I left the house in my tracksuit and Mum's raincoat and wellies.

I hadn't, at this point, linked back in with the friends, all two of them, who I had hung around with before heading off on my marital life. To be honest, I didn't want to. The town was small, and they probably already knew I was back given the way gossip tore around. It was part of the reason I struggled with the idea of going out and... what on earth would I say to anyone I knew anyway? The whole awkwardness. I imagined the creeping redness up my neck to my face and then the tears that I just didn't seem to be able to control. It wasn't something I was ready to endure.

Without a brolly I was quickly drenched, and I didn't see much bar the pavement. *Walking is good. Walking is good.* I played on repeat. *I am doing as I am told, and I am a good girl*. As I turned to go into the park I was abruptly greeted by a pair of feet.

'Excuse me but you should really look where you are going.' It was a slightly high pitched and annoying tone.

I didn't look up. Just shuffled forwards, trying to get around the voice. When I had taken a few steps further they spoke again, but it seemed I wasn't going to be getting away easily.

'Aggy?'

I stopped. Did I recognise the voice?

'Aggy is that you?'

I lifted my head slowly to see Molly, an old school friend. She looked radiantly orange, which I presumed was her tanning lotion. She had always been a big fan of this and the need to keep applying because it gave her a glow.

A half smile which was about all I could manage.

'Aggy what happened to you? You look so.... well...awful.'

I looked down, in part to hide the .... whatever was awful.

'Hi, how are you?' I managed.

‘I’m great Aggy. Oh, it’s been an amazing year, I’ve just had so much fun with James and we’ve got a baby on the way now so it just literally changes everything. We will never be on our own again. Can you believe it? I really can’t. Totally freaked me out and … gosh… what am I going to do with all these big clothes?’

She laughed, which was more of a shriek. I looked around to see if anyone was nearby who might be drawn to take notice of us. She was always destined to be successful; in terms of getting married young and making it successful and him being wealthy.

‘That’s great news…….’ I forced a smile. *‘I really must be going’* repeated in my head.

‘Oh, you’ll have to come to the baby shower and you just have to come round and see all the things we have for the baby already, it’s just so exciting. James has bought the most expensive cot and it is just divine. We’ve painted the nursery yellow because we don’t know if it’s going to be a boy or a girl of course. What about you come round this week? If you’re not doing anything of course, it would be lovely to see you. You could have some dinner with us. James has hired us a chef so it will be something good and healthy. You look like you could do with something healthy. I mean…. you look quite thin and pale. James would like me to have more people round, so we can show the place off a bit. It's quite big but that means we can have plenty of kids to fill it up.'

She shrieked again. 'Oh gosh I really must go, it's lovely to see you. See you soon!'

I'd been saved by Molly's haste. I watched as her glow slowly became smaller and then disappeared round the corner.

A water droplet trickled into my eye quelling the incoming surge of emotion of having seen Molly. I stood there, one eye shut, looking to see where I wanted to go next; wondering if I could actually be out of the house for more than an hour. I walked and breathed deeply. This was just a moment, in a day, in eternity. If this was so, I'm not sure I would seek out eternity.

There was a fork in the path which, if you followed it, did a full circle. I headed off to the left as nobody appeared to be on this stretch of path. The rain started to patter more heavily on my head and face, the water gliding down the back of my neck and inside the raincoat which was now redundant as it hadn't stopped the rain from breaking through. I found shade under a tree where a small bench was placed. Not one I remembered. But somebody else did. *'Bob's bench – 1921-2021.'*

I wondered if Bob would mind me sitting on his bench. But, since he wasn't around to tell me otherwise, and I had nowhere else to be, I sat and pulled the wet raincoat around me tighter.

It was chilly and I felt exposed. I wept. Quietly.

Eventually I calmed to wonder about the rain sodden grass in front of me, the paths which weaved their way around the grass, and the trees standing like markers. I thought about the days that had passed since I arrived back home. The emptiness had driven me to feeling numb and the view from where I sat was looking rather bleak.

It was the aroma of unwashedness wafting under my nose, that made me open my eyes. I was no longer alone. The smell was...well... I'm unsure how to describe it but something near a dead rat could be it. I shifted my eyes slowly to the side.

It was for sure a human being. Hagrid was all I could think. Hair and more hair and an ensemble of odd clothes all leading down to untied boots. I could see tainted flesh above the boots – an indication of the time lapse since a bath.

A young boy passed by on his scooter, 'Oi, Hagrid!' He gave a thumbs up as he whizzed by. I was not alone in my recognition. In hindsight, we may have looked like a suitable couple. It was still raining, I had nowhere to be and despite the smell, I didn't feel the urge to move. I felt suddenly warmer despite my damp clothing and my tears had found a distraction in human form.

Nothing passed between us but the smell. I could think of nothing else. I had every desire to move and head to the corner shop but instead I waited. What if the only person that I could befriend and sit with right now was an unhealthy-smelling tramp? How on earth had I got to this?

Somewhere amidst the curls of hair and beard, a sound came out. I'm not sure it was anything in particular, and I wasn't ready to ask. Making conversation was not something I was about at the moment. I shifted forward to stand up.

'See the shadows.' It was said with the succinctness of an actor. Every single letter heard.

I half turned to look at him but remained mute. I felt the need to move, but without having the capability of my body. A small butterfly of panic flew around my tummy and surged up into my heart. The fear exited in a multitude of tears. No control. Just an endless stream.

I could feel him, his eyes from beneath the curls, seeking out mine. What if I looked, would that mean something? I would have to speak then, and I so didn't want to. The time inched forward like an hour a second. We were hung in a space that didn't feel very comfortable at all.

Then he moved. Leaning in closer. I held still like a blinkered horse. The stench flowed full force towards me.

'The shadows round the trees.'

I swallowed as though a whole plum was going down.

'I don't understand,' I whispered back, still looking forward.

Nothing more came, it was like his message was complete. He pointed towards the trees in the distance, or whatever else was out there, and shuffled off having a mumbled conversation with himself.

As if unleashed, I headed swiftly off in the other direction to the park entrance. Back on the trail for the Vodka or whatever deal they had on in the corner shop that was seemingly my land of plenty. Far away from park benches and smelly tramps. I had to get home as quickly as possible. Everything was getting brighter, and the eyes of others were on me. If I made it to the shop, then I could make all of this go away. All I had to do was get there and then get home.

The corner shop was familiar. My breathing slowed. The rain had stopped and I had control back again. The comforting odour of fresh coffee wafted from the café next door. Intense and warm. I lingered and inhaled the air and the coffee before I entered the shop. Tightly packed, narrow aisles with my desired goods right at the back of the shop, I moved quickly along. The friendly labels came into view and an even better joy of the lower price tag almost had me weeping again. I paid with my crumpled ten-pound note and scuttled through the rain back to Mum's.

I don't recall the next hours, but suffice to say that there were times that I stood by the window and raised my glass 'to the trees.'

Chapter 4

Still

Tuesday again. It feels like I haven't slept much at all but I know that staying put will lead me to a very dark tunnel which I somehow manage to avert on awakening. So... what to do today? If I could do anything I would sit in the park. Maybe I could take Russian to the park with me? I smile at the idea. It's a plan at least.

It's bright today. I can see the dust layering the top of my tallboy. A few paw prints where Tiggy has been on there.

'Tiggyyyyy' I croak. 'Tiggggggyyyyy.' My books are on the floor – he's been up on the windowsill.

I shift to my elbows. 'TIG.'

He jumps up on the bed. 'Argh, Tig, you frightened me'. 'Have you been playing with my books again?' The purring and digging to get in close soften me, 'I know, you couldn't get on the bed............. It's okay.'

'AGNES!'

'Yes Mum!'

'Are you getting up?'

'Um...yes... I've got lots to do.'

'Oh?'

I can hear her going down the stairs. I'm awake that's enough.

As I sit up and pull the covers back, I notice a folded piece of paper next to the empty bottle of Russian. I don't recall putting it there. It has an old fashioned, yellowing look to it and a stamp on it. How odd. On closer inspection I can see something has been written just inside the fold. 'Follow the signs. See you soon. Lots of love. Bob.'

I search my memory of the previous night and can only find a frothy cloud of Russian. I must have picked it up on my way home. Then I recall the corner shop yesterday. The insistence of having a bag for my bottle. Yes, it was in the bag. Somebody must have left it in there.

Slightly relieved, but distracted by a wind rattling the windows, I climb out of bed. Then I feel the roar of my head.

Not sure I can dance with this Tigs. I tread gently down the stairs, one foot down, other foot down...next step.

Mum isn't patient at the best of times but today zero tolerance seems to be her level.

'I want to see this kitchen clean by the time I get home. No going out 'til you've done it. You need to get yourself down the job centre, and don't you go spending time at that corner shop,' with that, she was gone.

I stood still, in desperate need of a coffee, bed-hair wild. Fumbling through the cupboards, I find the coffee and also some painkillers, labelled for Mum, but good enough for me. I took two and went back to bed.

Chapter 5

In the Darkness

All was blissful. Until I was stirred by a dull thud and then the smell of her breath before I heard her speak. I had slept all day. These were the times I disliked the most, as she got into a rant about my inadequacies, which quite honestly wasn't particularly helpful and just upset her even more. After all, I was hers. Maybe she had dropped me on my head? Or perhaps she hadn't and that would make me the hopeless case I was without any cause.

'What have you done today? And how did you afford to buy that rubbish? Eh?'

I stood guiltily and meek. Peering at her blearily.

'Have you seen yourself? When are you going to learn?'

She stood and handed me a piece of paper.

'I suggest you get yourself here tomorrow.' She prodded at the piece of paper and slammed it on the table. I didn't see her go.

The water flowed down my throat into my nauseous belly. I felt hideous. More so than usual. And I had no idea how I had got through so much.

My head rested gently in my hands. *I can't stay here. I just can't. Not with her. Not with anyone.*

If it was possible to shake myself inside I would; well that was the feeling. I put my coffee cup somewhere that didn't offend the status quo of the gleaming kitchen. Steered myself back upstairs. Dressed. At least it was only just 5 o'clock. I pushed the clothes on the floor under my bed and left the house.

It didn't really occur to me until I was two streets away that it wasn't actually raining and I was dressed for a storm. The tears stung so I stopped moving. 'You are such an idiot!' I clawed the skin on my palms in the cave of my pockets. A maelstrom of emotion building inside me but suppressed by a short sharp shock. I stepped into the road. A sudden brush of air. I'm not sure if this was just before or just after the car passed me. And I held my balance ready to fall. Everything slowed in motion. The car had gone. I was stood in the road, in my wellies and raincoat, on a not-rainy day with crumbling insides. Had something odd just happened?

The tears that followed were of their own flow. They kept coming and I walked. I didn't stop walking despite the rubbing of the wellies, despite the wet warmth on my body, despite the glances and whispered comments, despite the hour.

I could see my breath in the light stream. I had cried enough and was just tired of having the same reaction to my inability to live a life. Nobody cared now and I certainly didn't. It wasn't funny. I was done.

'I need to leave now,' I whispered into the platform.

The station was deserted except for a person swaying around some distance away. Even they had given me a wider berth on passing, as if to confirm that I was doing the right thing. Only weirdos and drunks out at this time of night in Purbrey. There should be a warning for those sensible types who dared to venture out after 10.00pm.

The train was due in 5 minutes. My train for the trip out and no return. I didn't think anybody would notice if I was honest.

So, Agnes, what was your greatest achievement in life? What did you say? Oh yes, completely nothing..... you have achieved nothing. Only you don't get an Oscar for this. You get one for having a relationship, job, house, car, kids and all of those things that everybody else seems to manage so easily.

'Well, I can drink quite well actually, that's one good thing, yes?'

I took a large swig from the bottle I was gripping in my pocket. Might as well go out on form.

The monitor flashed, drawing my attention. It was 11:11. The train was late. Closing my eyes, I inhaled deeply. The station lights flickered before we were plunged into the night. I say we, as I was conscious of the person who had been wobbling at the end of the platform, only I could no longer see them. Darkness made it easier for me, as long as that person didn't move up this end. It wasn't a time to be interrupted. As I adjusted to the night and the moon light, I was pleased to see that I was alone...only to be disturbed again.

'Oi, what you doin'?' a voice from a distance interrupted my darkened silence. I stood still to avoid detection.

'You moron, d'you think I can't see you,' nobody responded. I took another swig.

There was laughter and then mumbles as the voices got further away. The last of the drunks from The Lion. Relief washed over me.

My air breaths had disappeared into the night. I heard a train signal passing in the distance and stood ready. A small parp, like a starter gun. I would know when to go and when was the right time. I shuffled to the yellow line, wiggling my toes as though I was feeling it before I stepped over it. Something about that felt quite good. I was over the line now, it was downhill from here.

I could feel something though. Like somebody watching or something getting closer. It struck me then that perhaps the person hadn't left the station. That they were watching. I looked around but couldn't see anything. No wobbling stranger. Nothing to see. And who would be at the station at this time anyway?

Back to stillness. My mind started to fill with naggings to reconsider. To stay put. What would happen to Mum when she found out I was gone? How would she deal with it? 'No.' I cried out into the dark. 'No.' Why should she get to keep me here?

A high-pitched twang and a fizzling sound followed by a reillumination of the platform and whole station, exposed my position very close to the edge of the platform. I panicked and took a step back, my heart thumping.

'This is an announcement. This station is now closed. There will be no further services running through this station today due to vandalism of the now cancelled 11:11. Please leave the station. There will be no further trains this evening, the next train to leave this station will be at 6.41am tomorrow.

I had failed. 'Shit... I can't even get this right.' I gripped my hand in anger, digging nails into flesh.

As I stepped back, I felt the cushioning of something or somebody nearby. The shame embracing me. Had somebody witnessed this whole thing? I turned quickly, almost losing my balance.

All thoughts ceased to come; all movements stunted. All I could do was exhale. I had failed.

Chapter 6

The Beginning

I arrived home, via the corner shop it seemed, given the rounded, cool bottle resting inside my coat.

I looked up to my window. The streetlight reflected in the glass. All I had to do was get past Mum.

'Agnes! WHERE have you been? Look at you. You are wet through. And you're wearing my coat that I haven't even worn yet. It's brand new. Didn't you think before you put it on?.'

The knives drove deep in one after the other. I held my breath. Clung the coat to me, with my hidden goods, and walked to the stairs.

'I'm sorry.' I whispered. Nothing else.

I left my wellies by the door – noting her sideways look and didn't wait for further verbal battering.

I wearily climbed the stairs and pushed into my room. Swigging from the bottle and laying back I faced the ceiling. *What had I almost done?*

Prickles tapped repeatedly on the back of my eyes. Knocking to come in... or out as it would be.

There was a random trill and Mum picked up the phone downstairs. The words seemed to seek me out. To taunt and make a point.

'She's been out, and I don't know where but, she looks bloody awful. I do wish she could pull herself together. Why she felt like she couldn't stay with Dan I do not know. She was set up very nicely there. I would've given my right arm for such a nice young man and a lovely house, and I know he would have looked after her to a ripe old age. I think she'll realise soon that the grass isn't as green as it looks Tracey. .... We've all had our difficulties of course yes and look how well we've done. I like my TV and little job. .... Exactly what I said.... And she will realise it's all....."

The conversation muted – either my choice or she had moved elsewhere.

I had done it all wrong.

You've done it wrong, you should've stayed with Dan. Yes, he said some things you didn't like, but you're sensitive. You're too sensitive. You're TOO sensitive.

I took a long swig. And savoured it. I wanted to be out of here. How could I have been so stupid.

A slight movement drew my attention to the floor. It was the piece of paper. Screwed up. I was sure I had put it in the bin. I took another swig and enjoyed the moment as I unfurled the piece of paper.

I searched my head for remembrance of this. Nothing. And who was Bob anyway?

The relief of Russian was winding its way as I laid back on the bed. It was a day not to remember and somehow this provided me with something to focus on and still my mind from the ravaging of the day. Where had I been? I relaxed into the 'no knowledge' and took deeper swigs. Closing my eyes allowed me to take pleasure, like sunbathing on a beach on my own. Warm and just......... nice.

A loud tap brought me back from the beach. I stood and went to the window. 'Is it you?'

The view from my window was unhindered. I could see both ways all along the street. The lamp outside lit up our pathway and small garden. A lone person walked past. Their shadow first behind then moving in front of them. Extending from their feet. They walked on.

A further tap encased my body in a momentary tenseness. Perhaps it was a bird or something dropping from the roof.

I surveyed the room but there was nothing to see. The water pipes, yes. This had happened before. Air in the pipes. I relaxed at my realisation. I was too tired now to consider any more options.

I needed to think of a plan to get out. To go. Though it did suddenly hit me that I had no money and I didn't particularly have any friends so how this could possibly work was beyond me. But me and Russian would sort it in a way that was unfathomable for the many. By the time he was empty we would be on a million-pound mission and a state of happiness would prevail. No more explaining where I was going, doing, or being. Just lots of niceness, as they would have to be to get any of the money from me. Can you imagine? How that could possibly be a life? Yachts, boats, champagne, a butler, a friend, a lover, a huge stash of Russian... ha!

You know what, I could be anything I wanted. I don't need the help of anybody else. It is going to be good. Lots of fun. Yes, lots and lots of fun. Created by me. The one everyone wants to be friends with Miss Agnes Wilderspin.

'I AM AGNES' came out a little too loud. Then quiet.

The tears started to flow.

I wasn't sure what came first. The bright red numbers or the sound. They both blared in a way. I did see the red, but the noise of the alarm made me jump. I turned to the clock and slammed down the snooze button.

11:11 shone brightly at me. Not in a violent way. But in a way that deserved acknowledgement. I was still grasping the piece of paper in my hand from earlier. Crumpled and damp I unfolded it. My heart beat a little faster. This was strange. Was I that drunk?

My whole body shifted an inch from the bed at the loud alarm noise again. After much fumbling around broken buttons, I turned it off. I straightened the clock. The numbers 11:11 still blazing. I held my breath for a few seconds. Was there flashing? Movement in between? The dictator of seconds?

The inactivity between the numbers caused inactivity in me. And then the flashing commenced, with my exhale.

I looked away and looked back to check. Still flashing.

Stumbling mentally through reasons and suddenly alert to the rest of my surroundings I sensed movement. Shifting round in hope of the cat, I was confronted with a parade of shadows playing on the clear wall.

I looked to the window. And then beside the window on top of the drawers I could see Tig sat watching the reflections. The streetlamp the projector, and the tree its film. Branches swaying, creating a live spectacle. A dance even.

I laid and watched. Their dance coming to life and looking like people all linked together in a sort of chain. Moving slowly. Then faster. Then a flutter as one seemed to break out of the link. It was mesmerising, calming, transporting me to a place that was more relaxed like watching a Newton's cradle.

CHAPTER 7

Presence

Darling Agnes. I was just sat here watching you as you slumber. Funny little pig snorts. So adorable. I have a plan for tomorrow that you will not be able to bring yourself to miss.

We……. This is in terms of you and me…….. we………. Will dance grandly. A little like this. Wiggle here, wiggle there. And then some head spins.

And a little like……

There is a thud as a book falls from the bed.

A pair of concerned eyes appear looking above the end of the bed.

Did you wake Agnes?

Ahem. So where were we? Today. Today we were healing. Today I was going to show you my magic tricks but then I realised we were at the station and it all got very difficult for me to, how does one say? I could not get your attention. I found a way and I really thought you saw me. But you were making one of those oceans again and alas I couldn't get past this.

See your beauty Agnes. See the way.

Anyway, I am leaving a little note for you.

Lots of super duper love

Bob

x

CHAPTER 8

A moment of pause

I woke suddenly. My mouth dry and my stomach churning. It was dark, bar the streetlight illuminating a circle on my ceiling. The coldness had penetrated my bones as I had been laid on top of the bed. I touched the radiator and it was surprisingly warm. I slid in under the duvet and cloaked it around me tight. Waiting for the warmth to grow. I could see the half-moon shape clear in the sky, which became masked by clouds then reappeared.

There was a creak and I noticed the door was open. Mum must've looked in. I felt a digging in my shoulder – another feather had popped out. I played with it for a while, the soft white strands lit by the outside light.

If I had a wish right now it would be... what would it be... I don't even know. Something to eat.

Creeping down the stairs at night wasn't something I usually did as the creaks were momentous. But my grumbling stomach was not abating.

Tiptoeing slowly from each edge I managed a few without noise but successfully made it to the bottom without any call outs to see if I was an intruder.

I popped some toast and found the remnants of marmite left in a small jar. Leaning against the sink I noticed the cat out in the back garden jumping every now and then. As if playing … though there wasn't anyone for her to play with. She bowed down as if to jump and then sat, watching, her head tilting from side to side.

The smell of charring toast pulled me back to the kitchen. I lacquered it with butter and marmite spreading it to the edges. The taste was a dream as I took a bite. Looking back to the garden I could see the cat on the fence now and staring upwards.

A creak alerted me and I turned around to see Mum.

'What you doing up?' she whisper shouted.

'Mmm.' I pointed towards the toast.

We stood in silence. Then saved by the startle of the cat flap as Tig bounced through as if being chased.

‘Bloody cat will be the death of me.’ She muttered and went off, followed by the cat.

I finished the rest of the toast, had a quick look for any leftover wine or sherry – to no avail – and mounted the stairs less carefully.

CHAPTER 9

Dream scape

My skin prickled with exposure to the cold air creeping in through the tiny gap at the bottom of my window. Filtering through into the dull emptiness that surrounded me. I wondered if I could make it through another day. But I hadn't managed to step off the precipice. And now, no sleep taunted me like a bully. My clock fuzzily shouted 3.00am in all its redness. I took a long breath. As I exhaled, tendrils of warm air filled the space in front of me. I did it again. Watching them float away towards the wall. I could see the branches of the tree on the wall. Waving this way and that. I stared, becoming lost in the simplicity of its lines. Watching it move gently. A fluttering disrupted the pattern. A fluttering? No birds are awake at night-time. A bat maybe. I had never seen a bat before in real life and waited to see if it swung upside down somewhere on a branch. A small smile creeping in at the illusion. I felt myself drifting into this.

The bat hung happily upside down on a long thick branch. Arms crossed. Swinging back and forth. Then, as if on command, it swung upwards and with a cord attached proceeded to flap flamboyantly around the wall, stopping at certain points. The trail of cord behind it being pinned here and there. Making lines, and shapes. Long and draping, both thin and thick, winding and straight. The bat looked now and then as if checking I was watching, checking that I was experiencing the artwork unfurling in front of me. A parade or performance just for me. And so it continued with line after line from the ceiling to the skirting. Finally, I started to see the shape of a giant tent. With a gathering at the top. The bat turned its back and made small movements around the top. I couldn't see what was happening, just arms and feet popping out; speedily and all around.

Further down I could see movement around the entrance to the tent. The flaps swung a little. An idea that there was life inside excited me. Life elsewhere. Life other than this one. Life not in this life. It suddenly struck me that this was just pretend. That I had no reason to be joyful or entertained. There was a shadow in the corner of the wall that seemed to be growing, starting to encroach on the edges of the tent. Not completely dark just a greyness creeping in and over. The uncertainty rose in my belly. A sense of something less good.

As I felt myself moving away from the joy of this creation coming to life, a head popped out of the tent flap. A hand came out also and waved. I wanted to wave back to let them know of this..... grey.... that was approaching. Nothing moved. Not my arms or hands. I tried to call out but just silence exhaled. I watched as the grey slowly consumed the whole tent. The head poking out from the tent, and the bat who managed to flap back to the tree and hang upside down and close its eyes. The flag he had been working on was now exposed. The letters stood out. Almost sparkled. Just for a brief moment. Before the grey consumed everything.

I woke to a thudding.

'Agnes. I'm going to work. Best you get up and get yourself to the bakery today.'

The heavy stomp on each bare wooden step echoed, as she descended.

I kept my eyes closed until I heard the gate clang closed. Barely able or wanting to open them to another day I laid and listened some more. There were cars. Passers-by mumbling and then some shouting. Children. Happy in their journey to school. The occasional cry and even a scream of the not so happy. And birds. I could hear them singing. Sat in the tree probably. Yes, in the same tree where the bat came from. I pondered this memory. My dream? Nightmare? I couldn't remember all of it just... yes... a bat somewhere in it. In my room. No, in the tree.

As I opened my eyes facing the wall, I could see feint marks. The tree branches reflected, this time by the sun.

Well at least it was sunny today. But, even so, I pulled the quilt in tighter around me. I wasn't quite ready for the day, though it was finding its way to me.

I laid, ear down, staring toward the wall. The clothes strewn on the floor just beside. Jeans and a t-shirt laid out ready to be put on. And something else just above the t shirt. It sparkled a little in the sunlight. I leaned on my elbow and screwed up my eyes to see if I could make out what it was. Just a piece of paper.

I swung my legs out of the bed to head to the bathroom. At least have a bath. Standing, I walked over to the wall and ran my fingers over the paint. Checking. Just to see if there was anything there. But no. Just the wall. No tree. No bat. Nothing else. I trampled on the clothes, bits of paper, and bottles, to the window. Yes. At least the sun was out today. I closed my eyes and breathed in some air coming through the gap in the window. I noticed then that something was stuck to my foot and reached down to rub it off.

Leaning against the wall I peeled off the paper. The sparkly writing. The reminder of my dream. 'Circus' it said. In bright red letters.

CHAPTER 10

First steps

I sat up in bed. It was ridiculously early. But I had no choice. Mum was loitering. Her intent on getting me out of the house had worked in a week's trial at the bakery. At this point I had only lingered outside briefly and salivated a little at the cakes. Today I got to serve them.

I anchored myself with a swig of Russian. Put on jeans and a t-shirt.

'Are you sure that's smart enough?'

'It's the bakery Mum, I can't see them wanting me to wear something too smart… I mean I'm going to be covered anyway with an apron and one of those nice hats.'

'Yes, but you should always dress above… oh it'll do.'

I hardly had a vast ranging wardrobe, so this was it.

It was the earliest I had left the house. There were people around and whilst it wasn't a big town, I felt strangely foreign. Maybe the hour or first day nerves? I had never worked in a bakery before. Actually, why on earth was I working in a bakery? I was used to working in an office. What could I bring to a bakery? I could eat the cakes for sure. But not so sure I wanted to.

As I scuttled past the school and bus stop, past the corner shop (which I might visit on the way back), I saw the store owner's son leaning in the doorway.

'Where you off to Ags?'

There was a wink and I felt slightly unnerved at the attention. I lowered my head, waved and carried on.

As I reached the bakers, I felt a sudden urge to turn around. This was not where I would normally work so why should I even go here now? I stopped still, not quite outside the shop front, and shuffled my feet. They seemed to have a mind of their own and were going back in the direction I had come. But we were interrupted.

'Agnes? Are you coming in?' It was sharp and uninviting.

I teetered on the edge of ignoring and striding off but something in me gave. Like a wind dropping after a major gust. I was in the door.

The smell of cakes and bread. I actually thought I could be turned at that point from Vodka to cake. It was delicious. I could literally taste and feel the sensation of the icing on those Belgian buns. I could have eaten them right now.

'Here's your apron. I'm Tracey, you'll be working with me on the counter today.'

I looked directly at her. She looked familiar.

I was brought back to reality and the fuzzy edge lost. I lifted the apron over my head and tied it off behind me. *What if I didn't know all the cakes?* The thought buzzed around like an unwanted wasp.

'All the breads are out. The prices are on the back of the tabs for the cakes. All of them are separate on the screen so you can't go wrong. Just make sure you put in the right size for the breads sometimes that's a bit confusing and the buttons don't work...'

The conversation went on about cakes and bags and bread that could be cut in the cutting machine which had different settings. The 3 tables that needed wiping down after people left. And the front glass also after kids had put their fingers all over it.

'You need to wash your hands. And then put these on.' She flung a pair of lycra gloves at me.

'Make sure your apron's on properly too.' She shifted the neck around and fiddled around the back of me undoing and redoing the bow.

'And put your personal belongings out the back. You won't need them. You will need to wear a smarter top tomorrow, you're not lounging about.' It stung but I was still a little numbed.

'Whereabouts should I put them?' a shamefully timid utterance wandering from my mouth.

'Ask Ruth.' Tracey gestured towards the kitchen.

I almost left there and then but instead decided to seek out Ruth in the hope she was somehow a bit less sharp. That the knives that had landed in words since arrival were not a sign of things to come.

As I went into the kitchen area, I saw a round and red-faced woman shovelling something in to her mouth.

'Ooof, ... shorry...' she chewed frantically and wiped her mouth.

'Sorry, are you the new girl?'

'Yes. I um.. where do I put these?' I raised my bag and coat.

‘Just over here,’ she smiled, showing off bits of moistened cake stuck in her teeth.

I liked her already.

The day spun from catastrophic - as I stuck my finger randomly in cakes whilst pointing at them - to nightmare - as I poured weak tea - and ended with cleaning icing repeatedly off tables. I had decided that doing as I was told and focusing on the end of the day would get me through.

Stepping out of the door at the end of the day, with a glare from Tracey followed by a reminder about my t-shirt, I didn’t know if I could possibly come back the next day. Ruth’s cakey smile from the kitchen door made it a possibility. I knew though that I would head to the corner shop and see if they could loan me a bottle. I didn’t really care what it cost.

I was just around the corner when Mum appeared from the corner shop. She looked surprised and then not so happy to see me. The opportunity was missed to turn back I continued towards her.

‘So did you manage to get through the day?’ She looked me up and down as if checking I had visited a place of work. Or was it a look of disgust? I couldn’t be sure. I needed a drink.

‘Yes, I’m feeling tired.’ I had a little bit of frost in my own voice.

‘Not used to working my girl. You’ll get used to it.’

We walked together. An odd occasion.

‘I spoke with Dan today,’ she bristled.

I had a sense it was not going to be a joyful conversation.

‘Mum, I’ve just finished work….’

‘He said he wanted to try but you just weren’t interested… He was upset you left, but said you were drinking a lot.’

I could sense her looking even though I kept my gaze forward.

‘Well?’ she demanded.

‘What Mum?’

‘He’s a good man, what’s wrong with you? You must stay and try at these things you don’t just wake up and decide, ‘not today’. I said you were a silly girl and if there’s anything he needed he was to let me know.’

‘Mum I can’t have this conversation now.’

'It's about time you started to take a look at yourself. Surprised you even got up for work. You could've been in a nice house, with a lovely young man and all set up for the future.'

'Mum, I have to go.'

'It was such a wonderful opportunity and I think he's a lovely young man – why do you have to take the difficult route each time Agnes?'

There was a silence that I couldn't fill, and she looked as though she might cry. The pricking sensation at the back of my own eyes was an indicator of my need to find space.

I walked away, head down, feeling her thoughts delving into my back, head and heart. A stream of judgement on my ungracious actions that lead to my current state.

Let the court be seated for the sentencing of Agnes Wilderspin. Don't think, don't think, don't think.

The park beckoned. It was the only place that felt like it didn't judge me. Didn't question what I was doing next. What I did for every single moment of the day.

As I stepped into it, I felt the sun reach out its tendrils to warm me. Taking away the need to hurry. I walked, trying not to think but somehow thinking. I found the bench and sat.

Was it me? I was all wrong. I should have stayed. But then... what then?

There was a rustling and then the intense smell. If I hadn't known better, I'd have thought he was following me. He grunted as he sat. A faint whiff of pee wandered my way. I wondered when the last bath had happened and ... well... the thought of getting him in the bath at Mum's. I smiled because it made me want to laugh out loud. *Hi Mum, meet Hagrid, he's come to the use the bath.* What would she say to that? Or maybe she wouldn't because it would be too much to say something to somebody that she had never met before.

He grunted again. A sort of throat clearing with a puff out of his mouth. Sometimes with a horsey lip tremble.

'I started a job today,' I offered into mid-air.

A slight nod of acknowledgement.

'At the bakery.'

He fingered his chin's curly mass. Stroking it with consideration.

'I'm not sure about the people, well, one in particular, but ……. there's a funny girl there… I like her.'

Nothing else followed. We sat and listened to the silence until dusk started in and I knew that I had to head for the corner shop, put a bottle of Russian on tab and head home.

'Where are you staying tonight, Hagrid?'

Still ruffling his beard. 'I just might stay here.' His tones were mumbled but considered.

That was it. Nothing else. And I didn't feel I should ask more. After all, I didn't want to explain myself to anyone so why should I expect Hagrid to?

CHAPTER 11

Seeing in the dark

My head vibrated as I sat up. Still, I got myself ready. Screechy redness was telling me it was 6.05 and if I didn't move quickly, I would be late for my second day.

There was a crispness in the air which I allowed into my unbuttoned coat. To allow it into my bones almost so that it would distract me. I felt like I had walked with my eyes shut. Outside the bakery in a split second, or so it seemed, I stood and wondered … to go in…. to not go in. Tracey was already getting things ready.

Her head appeared outside. 'Morning, hope you had an easy night. There's lots to do, the bread's almost ready. Make sure the tables are cleared and get yourself a clean apron, that one shouldn't even be seeing the light of day.' She gestured with her thumb aiming behind her.

My day was marred by a heavy head and tense glares from Tracey. I smiled and spoke courteously to customers despite their sometimes clipped and ungiving communication. I suppose it was easy to point and say, 'that one'.

After the fog had cleared, I noticed an older couple who had been in the previous day and sat in. Tea and cake. He, with the biggest cream doughnut and her, with a cherry tart. I wondered if this was their daily outing. Their obvious years were additionally characterised by his hand tremor and her nodding head. A kind of pantomime in real life. I loved them immediately from this view. They talked silently.

My people watching was interrupted by a sharp instruction from Tracey, 'Tables need clearing.' I moved like an automaton. Programmed to do as instructed.

My duties brought me closer to the couple as they slurped their tea. Their cakes finished, I went to move their plates. His trembling hand reached out to stop and keep the plates there, 'Betty hasn't finished yet.'

The tone was gentle and I paused for a moment looking at the empty plates but decided that if they weren't ready that was ok. I placed them back down on the table. I felt Tracey's eyes on me. I sensed if I took the plates I might get some sharper talk from the elderly couple and if I didn't, a complete ruination from Tracey.

I decided that Tracey was worse. 'I'm so sorry ... Betty... .' I hoped the recognition may help. 'Can I get you another tea or something else; more cake, or a cake to take home?'

The man looked at me as if I had stepped off a spaceship.

Betty reached a veiny hand over to cover the equally lined hand of her companion. 'Albert, shall we go dear?'

'We don't want anything else thank you, just to be left in peace.' His tone was shaky but firm.

I felt the heat rising, the taste of bile, and the need to exit to fresh air in whichever way possible. My moment of statue practice gave Betty an opportunity to smile a non-toothy smile. At that point I moved in a fast walk, back behind the counter, without the plates and out to the kitchen and to the toilet. *This was never going to work. I can't even work in a bakery*. I wretched over the toilet trying to limit the noise. This was not going well.

I heard a gentle knock. 'Agnes... want some water?' Ruth's childish tones echoed through the door.

My red face and watery eyes greeted her cakey grin. Smiling through my discomfort, I gratefully took the glass.

‘Sorry… not very good for a second day… I just…’

‘It’s ok, it’s your nerves.’ She leaned in whispering ‘and her ladyship has the whip out today.’ I felt some comfort from her quirky understanding but what I needed was not to be here.

‘I don’t feel well at all, I might have to go home.’

Ruth wrapped her hands over her belly and smiled, with a closed mouth this time.

‘I think you need to take up cake eating with me. Better than anything else. Cakes don’t smell so much.’

I felt her referencing my drinking. Or perhaps it was a slight blink of paranoia?

‘I’m not sure what you mean. I think it’s a bug. I’ll be okay I just need to drink plenty of water today.’

She nodded. I took a big slug of the water.

The rest of the day I spent on autopilot. Couples came in and went. It seemed to be a day of people exposing their amazing relationships. Tracey’s husband came in and gave her a kiss even though she glowered at him. It seemed she did this a lot. It got me thinking though. *Even Tracey can do it.*

I watched out of the window, as couple after handholding couple, bounced down the street announcing their togetherness to the world. Happy ever after. Something that I hadn't managed and yet everyone else seemed to.

'Are you working today or window shopping?' Tracey's sarcasm filtered into my dream world.

I busied myself and went to get the remaining bread from the kitchen. On return, I noticed a figure I knew at the window looking in at the cakes.

'Oh my word, he better not come in here or we'll have to fumigate. How on earth do people allow themselves to get like that?' Tracey moved from behind the counter and stepped into the doorway.

'Move along... go on... off you go.'

Hagrid looked up and our eyes met. I saw something of a smile underneath the mass of curly beard. With a half-smile back I hurried to clear the tables, avoiding any eye contact with Tracey in case she had seen.

'Shoo.... before I get my broom out.' I actually laughed. Though I felt sad for Hagrid I think he probably wouldn't care too much. Somehow, his presence had made me feel good.

'Right, now the smell's got rid of, let me see how you are serving.' Just the thought of her watching me serve made my stomach twist.

She stood back and opened her arm out – welcoming me to my apparent audition which I was destined to fail.

An older man came in. 'Hello Arthur.' She smiled knowingly and then looked at me and nodded.

And here we have Agnes about to make the biggest mess in the history of cake serving, but that's okay because she's pretty useless at everything else anyway.

'What can I get you for..... I mean... for you,' I stumbled.

Arthur's needs were simple. He wanted a middle piece of bread pudding. I took small glimpses at Tracey, more to check how close she was than anything, and could sense her growing irritation.

I found the tongs and then, after a while looking for the bread pudding and being guided by the finger of the Arthur, I delved straight for the very middle piece. Not the end middle piece. No, the very middle. I managed to destroy the end piece anyway by which point Tracey had whipped the tongs out of my hand.

'Let me do it. She's just started Arthur, you know what these youngsters are like.' For me, her tone switched to pointy. 'Agnes. Watch carefully.'

I felt the heat rise at the same time as the little contents I had in my stomach. I glanced at Arthur who watched Tracey deftly pick up the piece of bread pudding and slide it into a bag without it touching the sides.

'Perfect. Thank you, Tracey.' He nodded to her and was on his way. I was apparently invisible.

I mumbled something about needing the toilet and headed into the kitchen area where I was able to breathe and get something to drink from my bag.

The rest of the day slid by. Filled with more smiles, lots of table cleaning, and a reminder that this was actually a probationary period, and it would be reviewed at the end of two weeks so I needed to keep up 'the improved effort,' it felt like home from home.

CHAPTER 12

Patterns

I exhaled like a deflating balloon as I left the shop.

The walk home was not as speedy as the one to work. I pondered an evening without comfort. It wouldn't be easy. I would have to sit with Mum and watch TV and feel her intense judgement.

Too much already, I crossed the road and turned to the corner shop. The old couple were just emerging with a bag of what looked like bottles. I kept my head down and swept past them. I didn't look up but noticed they stood still from the corner of my eye. I felt their eyes watching as I moved away. Probably muttering to themselves at how stupid that girl in the bakery had been today.

I decided that something was needed and went into the shop on a kind of conveyor belt feeling. I saw Billy behind the counter. His eyes peeling along as I walked to the back.

Would he allow me it on tab?

I didn't want him to think I was… well… an alcoholic. People make assumptions and I didn't drink in the morning anyway.

I rummaged in my handbag in hope that there was some random note lurking at the bottom. The last time I cleared it out wasn't available in my memory but was evidently some time ago. I put it on the floor and unloaded each individual item; receipt, hanky, pen, mint, raisin. Just like the golden ticket – crumpled up in a corner was a note. I looked closer. Unfolding it crease by crease and picking off bits of old raisin the £5 note smiled at me.

What could I get for a fiver?

I piled all the remnants back into the bag and looked excitedly to find, not my usual, but a sufficiently golden bottle of wine. I carried it proudly to the counter.

'Afternoon Agnes.....' he sung out.

I continued to look down. 'Hi.'

'I'd like to walk with you but the boss is out. Next time maybe?'

The silence was too long and I couldn't see my bottle heading back to me so I had no choice but to look up.

He winked and handed me the bottle protected by a thin bag. I reached out to take it but was stalled by his hold. 'Well? Can I walk with you another time?'

'Maybe.' My redness pulsated so wildly I yanked the bottle from his hand and walked quickly out of the shop.

As I opened Mum's front door, I could hear her talking in the kitchen.

'I'm just so sorry but you know what she's like. Not one for sticking at things. Never has been. I don't know what she thought she was doing....... No......... of course, it's not your fault at all Daniel. Anything I can do please say, I mean it's no trouble. Keep in touch won't you.'

I contemplated walking back out the door. But wondered if that would mean not sticking at things. And I had nowhere else to go anyway. I'm not sure who was more disappointed.

I crept up the stairs, into my room, locked the door, and wept.

CHAPTER 13

Connection

Was I awake? It was cold again though and I could see my breath. My clock light shone out loudly. It was 3.00am exactly. Still dark. Too early to be awake. I had work in 4 hours. My breath seemed to swirl, caught in the light peeling in from the streetlamp. Bright and luminous with no curtain to hinder its way. It struck me that the shadows were swaying. It must be windy outside. All the leaves fluttering. And then some floating off to the ground. As I watched lazily, the shapes on the wall started to move more. Slowly at first. I didn't quite see it until a redness seemed to seep in. Like an invisible artist at work, I watched as the intricate lines and colours formed. The smoothness of pace and drawing of each line was as though it breathed its own life force.

I watched intrigued as the bat appeared. An eruption into life form, as it set about taking the lines, flowing and draping, gracefully and with intention. Then filling with shades of intense colour. Red sections, interspersed with white. Flowing down the first layer and then a longer second layer to the skirting. It felt like I was part of the construction of a puzzle though my hands were not piecing this. In its full form it resembled a huge tent, maybe, yes, a circus tent. The big top. I'm sure I had read a book or seen this somewhere years ago. For now, I wasn't interested in that though. I was waiting to see what came next. There were flickerings and flappings as the edges of the tent were seemingly pinned into the skirting. Firmly in place. And then nothing. Or maybe, was that a twitching of the entrance flap?

I floated out and then back in again. Wakened by the hint of a sugary smell, gently teasing my nostrils at first. It wasn't an unusual smell. And it was warm. Candyfloss? I breathed in deeply. Feeling the warmth of the soft pink. Opening my eyes fully I could see a candyfloss machine parked right by the entrance to the tent. A wheeled trolley and on it the central clear plastic allowing the sight of the pieces of soft fluff sticking randomly to the sides. A gentle hum stirring. I could feel the fluff dissolving in my mouth. A slight bubbling and then it was gone. Followed by the desire for more.

Leaning on my elbows I could take in the whole picture. Further up I was sure I could see the entrance flap slightly open. And yes, there looked to be somebody peering out again.

The shriek of 6.00am had my body lift from the bed about two inches. Had I slept? I moved without thought. Legs out swinging up. Swinging down. Quilt back over. Repeat. This time I opened my eyes to the face the wall.

Just a dull red smudge, existed.

No time to think of my foggy head and parrot cage mouth. I moved just the minimum. I managed to be dressed and teeth done. Then I walked. The birds wildly shouting to be heard for miles and miles. I quite enjoyed their tunes. It woke me graciously. No questions. No queries. No disputes. Just birdsong and me. It reminded me of a kind of freedom, which ignited something in me but I was unsure what. All I had to do was wake up before I got to the bakery and be ready for Tracey.

Today's walk was a little different though as there was something going on outside the corner store. My supplier. Ha! Maybe they were supplying something else? As I got closer, I saw Billy stood in the doorway watching as his father argued with a delivery person. I slowed. Unsure if perhaps I should say something as it seemed quite a loud exchange. But what would I say? 'This man has given me free Russian Proud for the last two weeks don't you dare speak to him that way.'

No. Perhaps, 'You shouldn't talk to him in that way.' No, not that either. In fact, I decided it was best to cross the road and, as I stood waiting, I felt a presence beside me, and a waft of aftershave. What was it with smells?

'May I walk you to work young lady?'

I realised I hadn't bothered with make-up and felt suddenly conspicuous.

I looked down and mumbled. 'No not this morning, I'm in a hurry.' I sped up a little to make this real.

He continued to walk alongside me.

'You know, it would be great to see you smile in there.' He offered, matching my step.

Even if smiling were a thing at 6.00am I wasn't sure I would be able to do it. I was beginning to feel those bubbly feelings and my breath was getting shorter. I had nowhere to hide.

But then he took two quick steps in front of me. 'Agnes?' I stopped as he did a forward roll, stood up, and bowed. Right there. On the hard ground. Turning to face me with a wide grin on his face.

I smiled and stifled a laugh. 'What are you doing?' I was momentarily bemused but also conscious of anyone who might have seen.

'Made you smile didn't I? Job done.' He winked. 'I think you should let me take you out for a coffee and a cake after work. No... she says.... do not show me a cake after a whole day of looking at them. Ok then I shall bring you some fruit. It's good for you and it won't just be any fruit, it will be the best in the land.'

He laughed to himself, stuffed his hands in his pockets, and swaggered alongside me for the rest of the journey without uttering a word.

As we reached the bakery he stopped and bowed. 'I shall see you later lovely lady.'

My mouth was slightly open, not sure if I should have responded but also realising that I didn't think there was a choice. I would be seeing him again. I liked it.

CHAPTER 14

Finders Keepers

The day went like a snail having naps. Tracey was in a bad mood and I didn't make this any better by putting the trays in the wrong way round and putting the labels on incorrectly. I knew what a Belgian bun was but today it became an Éclair.

Ruth winked at me from the door as Tracey painstakingly explained the difference between the two cakes with exasperated huffs at the idea that I didn't know which was which. I didn't offer any explanation. My mind had been elsewhere but this would not help my cause.

Somebody had taken the time to make me smile this morning and nothing else was touching me. I felt almost untouchable. And all because of a roly-poly. This on any other day would have caused a panic. A non ability to cope or just be. A need to run and hide. But not today. It almost made me feel *special*. But I couldn't think it too loud. Just in case.

Betty and Albert, as I now knew them, were in as usual. Same table, same cake, same tea. Same look for each other.

‘How are you both today?’ I broke their gaze. ‘We’re just ….fine,’ Albert offered breathing deeply but smiling like a man who has caught his biggest fish.

Betty looked at me intently. ‘You look very rosy today dear. Nice to see that smile.’ They turned back and gazed at each other – nobody else in their world.

I took extended time cleaning tables after lunch, trying to eek out time, so I could go home and have a nice refreshing something or other to end the day. People left things behind almost every day. Mostly dummies or toys. Sometimes keys – but people would come back for those.

Today I found a soft elephant in the corner. Worn but pretty pink. I brushed it off and went to take it to the kitchen. As I turned, I was confronted by a wrinkled t-shirt.

‘Still okay for later.’

I felt a warm glow creep up my neck and face. A little weirded out by him turning up again.

‘Mm hmm.’

‘I will be back for you later lovely.’ He did a spin, winked and went out the door.

Tracey stood with her hands on her hips.

'What was that all about?'

I shrugged and headed to the kitchen with the pink elephant – somewhat unsure what had really happened then.

Ruth looked wide eyed at me just before she popped in the rest of a piece of bun. 'Shee yuv gorrun admira'.

I felt myself glowing again.

'Ssh, no he's not'. *Why are you shushing her Agnes*?

I felt the warmth of Tracey behind me.

'Come out and serve please. What's that you've got? Now I've seen it all – you have to bring a cuddly toy to work?'

She whipped it from my hand and stuffed it in the drawer.

Re-entering the front shop I noticed there was nobody there. Puzzled I turned to Tracey.

'I need to have a word with you about that young man. He's no good.' She tapped her head at this point, which I wasn't sure if it was her wiping something off or referring to him being a little not right in the head.

Shaking her head and looking down her nose, 'He's never around for very long you know. Trouble. You don't want to be getting caught up with them types. He can't even iron his shirts. And his family own that corner shop where there are some very strange things going on – I've seen the men there collecting things. I bet you it's drugs. Just you be careful. I can put a stop to him coming in here.'

Slightly bewildered as to where this had all come from, I just nodded.

'I'm sure your mum won't like him. In fact, it would give her a heart attack.'

I almost laughed but stifled it with a cough. It wasn't even funny. I knew she was right. Mum wouldn't like somebody 'like him.'

The afternoon crawled by. We cleared the remaining cakes and cleaned. One eye on the door and one on wiping down. I felt odd flutters. These diminished and grew into some form of disappointment as Tracey shut and locked the door behind me. I stood and looked up and down the street. Had I expected something different?

I headed slowly home. Now with a diversion to the supermarket, as I didn't want to go into the corner shop. Maybe I hadn't looked so good today. And I hadn't said much when he came in. I should have been more chatty.

But you're not chatty Agnes. You're sad and quiet.

He wouldn't want to be around me. I wouldn't want to be around me. I wandered heavily in the direction of the supermarket. Focusing on the ground in front of me.

It didn't really matter. Who was he anyway? And Mum wouldn't like somebody like that.

I concentrated on my best idea for a night in and the fact that I could afford a bottle today. Even though I would rather have had some real company. Maybe I *could* go to the corner shop. At least I knew they sold my favourite there. But what if he was there? It would be awkward. *I* would be awkward.

'Penny for 'em?'

I looked up startled. Confronted by a crumpled t-shirt, a smile and wink.

'I…….' lost for words I looked down.

A glimmer of concern in his eyes. 'You thought I stood you up?'

My eyes were momentarily glazed but fingernails in my palms took away the sting.

'No… not at all… it …. It wasn't a date,' I laughed falsely

'But you wanted it to be...,' another grin. He circled his arm in mine. Moving forward without thought, my original destination detoured, we stood at the edge of the park.

'You don't have to worry so much you know. It's already sorted. Look at this… .'

I watched as he planted a hand on the ground and seemingly plugged himself into it and hovered easily. A little embarrassed, I prodded the grass with my foot, looking away from Billy's acrobatics. I wondered what Hagrid would say if he walked by now. Not sure anything would surprise him. Might even make him laugh which happened about random things.

'Oi, are you watching?'

The show continued. This time with cartwheels. One after the other. I was beginning to feel self conscious at being the only spectator. The park was strangely quiet. Even though the sun was out and it would normally be busy because of schools finishing.

'What do you think?' he rubbed his hands as he walked back towards me. An air of self-confidence moulded itself around Billy.

'You're really good.... Where did you learn to do all of this?' I asked.

'I taught myself.' His smile was both naïve but warm and kind.

'Not everyone can do this you know. I could teach you. It's simple.'

I looked away. I hardly did any exercise let alone a cartwheel which I probably did last when I was about 11 years old. Or maybe 13, given that I was still playing with marbles at this point while everyone else was getting more engrossed in their mobiles.

Billy did a trail of cartwheels again. This time a couple walked by and watched. The audience presence seemed to will him on even more as he did a handstand and stayed there for what seemed like an eternity. He returned to feet down and the couple applauded.

'Good on you mate – I couldn't do that,' the guy offered. Billy returned to me smiling.

'Let's go and sit on the bench.' He pointed to Bob's bench. I felt a bit unnerved in case Hagrid appeared. It felt kind of disloyal but I didn't know how to put this into words. Especially when Billy was already steering me. So I slowed in resistance.

'Come on – I've got something for you.'

'For me?' Distracted, I allowed myself to be guided.

He winked.

I sat and watched while Billy fished around in his rucksack which was all patches. Unusual. Much like him really. Eventually he found what he was looking for at the bottom of the bag.

'Here.' He held out his open hand containing a daisy brooch.

It wasn't mine. And yet I took it and held it in the palm of my hand. The petals were long and graceful. Pure white and perfectly circling the intense yellow.

'You dropped it in the shop a couple of weeks ago. My Dad had it on the counter but forgot to give it to you.'

'It's... it's not mine.'

Billy looked directly into my eyes. Looking to see something. Checking to see if I was for real, maybe. Uncomfortable I looked away.

'It is now.' He wrapped my hand around the brooch. 'Finders keepers yeah. Sometimes things are meant for us even though we think they aren't. The person who had it doesn't need it anymore 'cause they would have come to pick it up by now.'

We sat for some time without talking. This seemed to happen a lot on Bob's bench. Maybe Bob was mute. We were sort of held in a moment. I didn't want to break it. The feeling was warm and nice.

'If you could do anything you wanted to... what would it be?'

His question caught me off guard. Had he asked me a couple of weeks ago I would have suggested the end of this life. This seemed far away from the moment I had reached now.

'I don't know. What about you?' I deflected it to him.

He looked at me questioningly but looked away, clearly deciding not to pursue the thought.

‘I’m going to run away and join the circus.’

I looked at him quizzically. Then he smiled. Nudged me. And proceeded to show me how to do a cartwheel broken down into three easy steps.

The rest of the day was filled with more laughter than I had ever remembered…. Ever.

CHAPTER 15

Circus

Mum was sat in her same position. Same sallow expression which sapped my energy as soon as I walked through the door.

'What time d'you call this?'

'I met a friend.'

'Anything could've happened to you.'

'I'm 32 Mum I'm not a child.' My response startled both of us. She looked back at the TV and we didn't speak again that day.

I got in to bed with a warm feeling. Memories of the afternoon with Billy and his endless energy and total disregard for what anybody else thought rang through me like a new tune. It had been a good day. A smile spread across my face.

The tree swayed outside despite no wind. The moon lit up the branches on the wall and then the bat flew swiftly in, hanging momentarily upside down. I had one eye open waiting to see if there was to be any drawing. I wasn't disappointed.

Swinging. Flapping. Hovering. I found myself inside the circus tent of the previous dream. This time the colours started to fill inside. The red and white on the large drapes. The wires of the trapeze and the abandoned unicycle at the very centre of the circle. I watched as the bat started to draw wildly in one space. A red nose, wild curly hair, braces, giant shoes all coming to life. The bat flapped away and hung upside down again. One eye open.

Nothing moved. The silence piercing. So much so that I was startled by the giggle that came. The largest smile of the clown took up space as he stood up and then did cartwheels all around the ring. Back flips were next, leading him to the centre and to the unicycle where he stopped and considered. Contemplated. He held up the unicycle. First by the wheel, then by the pedal, then by the seat. The realisation dawning that this was how it would work he tried every way; jumping up, launching himself, climbing but to no avail. Sad. He walked away to the back of the tent and reappeared moments later with a set of steps. Big smile. Cocking his leg over he wiggled this way and that. Fell backwards. Forwards. Finally, balance came. He tore round and round the ring waving madly and blowing kisses to all the invisible spectators. He was having the time of his life.

Leaning forward he dropped gracefully from the unicycle and bowed deeply. His index finger extended towards me. Followed by frantic beckoning which had his arms spinning wildly. I hesitated.

In my pyjamas…. Really?

The pull was magnetic. I appeared to have no ability to resist and allowed myself to be transported. I was next to the large red smile and enormous eyes in a blink. Seconds later, I was at the top of the steps putting my leg over to get on the seat. And then my feet on pedals with my arms out wide like a balance pole. I looked out to the invisible spectators who cheered with encouragement. With effortless poise I was off. Gathering speed as I went round and round the ring. Drinking in the endless applause and the most freeing feeling that I was flying.

Everybody cheered as I pedalled backwards. Stood still and balanced. And off round the ring again swerving this way and that.

A glorious time of an out-pouring of love just for me. For Agnes. Waves and waves of emotion, pouring.

Then just one moment. I felt a wobble. My heart did its own dance. I didn't feel so balanced. Something was wrong and I needed some help, some reassurance. Where was the clown? Where was .... everybody? All I could see were rows of empty seats. All the lights were out except for one dull lamp at the centre of the ring. I had to get to it. Somehow this was everything. The help, the reassurance all sat in this one little ring of dull light. A loud click echoed around the tent followed by an intense blackness as all light was extinguished.

CHAPTER 16

Gifts

I woke suddenly. The duvet half on the bed and little on me. I shivered and pulled it back up to wrap around me. Had I been dreaming? All I could remember was a clown and a smile. A stupidly big painted on smile. Billy ram raided into my thoughts. It gave me a warm feeling that made me smile…. a stupidly big smile as it happens. I felt good.

Taking time to get ready in the morning was foreign to me, but today I had the time and whilst my clothes were limited and I was going to be wearing an apron, I still looked for something nice. Something I hadn't worn. Emptying the pockets of yesterday's jeans, I came across the daisy. I clasped it in my hand for a moment. Pondering yesterday afternoon.

Sometimes things are meant for us even though we think they aren't.

It fitted well with the crazy patch like effect on my top. Looking at myself I wondered if I was actually me. I mean, who was this girl dressing herself up?

You look good.

I winked at myself and glanced towards the door. Could I be a little bit pretty?

I took my cups down to the kitchen and put them in the dishwasher, then swept out of the house quickly. No interaction.

6.00am and all was well. Some cars as usual. The sun was emerging through some clouds. And as I walked I looked around as people who had early starts walked and drove by. As I looked they looked back. I smiled. They smiled back. Like they were in on the secret. Whatever that might be.

As I passed the corner shop I looked hopefully. The door was closed. As I looked closer, I could see the owner shifting boxes around inside. No Billy. It was early though and I was sure to see him during the day.

Friday was always good at the bakery. Both because Tracey wasn't there and also because it was Friday and I didn't work a Saturday.

Ruth was already at the counter placing one cake on the tray and putting one in her mouth. Or it seemed like that. She was oblivious to me stood at the door. I knocked hard and watched her spit out a little cake as she was startled. Not very hygienic but Tracey wasn't around to pick up on it. We both laughed. Which lead to further cake bits exploding.

Our morning was littered with similar incidents. Customers were happier. They left big tips that weren't usually offered at all. Miraculous. As it came to lunch time my attention turned to Billy. He hadn't dropped in yet. I felt a little deflated, but this was soon dismissed as I had a huge influx of secondary school kids looking for a sugar fix. One of the kids winked at Ruth which had her flush so red I thought she might explode. They cheered as she ran out to the kitchen at the back to hide. As the queue dissipated, nearly all the cakes were sold. Only one Belgian bun remained.

'Has that one got my name on it?'

I looked up to the crumpled t shirt and smiled.

'It has and we are giving it away today.' Did I really say that out loud?

A wink, and he went to sit at a table.

Ruth and I cleared everything in record time, cleaned the kitchen ready for the morning and ensured that there were no crumbs left on the floor from the earlier explosions. Tracey would not be very welcoming if there was a hint of a crumb out of place.

As I headed back into the seating area Billy was stood by the door. He seemed distracted for a moment by something in his hand, a piece of paper. I nudged the cabinet door to let him know I was there. He folded the paper and put in his pocket. Grabbed my arm, looped his through, and off we went.

Walking with Billy was more of a jaunty style. I felt like Dorothy in Wizard of Oz if we got into step.

As yesterday, he steered me to the park. There were more people around and after a turn of cartwheels and handstands he insisted on getting me to try.

'Come on - give it a go. I'm here. I'll catch you so you won't hurt yourself. Promise.'

After a few attempts, hands on the ground, upside down. I had a view of Billy's world in that afternoon in the park. People looked on. Some with raised eyebrows. Some with smiles. Some with interest. All in a very different world for ten seconds. I imagined just being that way always. Seeing that different view.

'You're a natural. You don't need me to help you.'

'Yes I do, I couldn't do it on my own.'

'You can do anything Agnes. Anything. Honest.' Billy got some plums out of his rucksack.

'Want one?' I shook my head and watched as he sunk his teeth into the plum and a little juice ran down onto his t-shirt. He brushed it and carried on.

'See you've got the brooch on. Looks good on you. Somebody came in the shop today asking for it but I said it had a new owner.'

'You didn't!'

'I did. I gave them your address too but said.. you know... finders keepers.'

'But Billy... it's not mine... ' I struggled to take it off with shaking hands. Mortified that I had what would be stolen goods.

Billy laughed, uncontrollably. Almost spitting plum at me.

'Are you joking?'

He looked with some seriousness and a smirk.

'Sometimes we are given things we just can't give back, because they belong to the person in a way that it's part of their jigsaw yeah. Bit like love really.'

I didn't know what to say. Still unsure if I was wearing somebody else's brooch but also with a feeling of warmth coming over me.

'It's a good thing Agnes. Keep it. It'll remind you of me.' Again, he laughed raucously.

We stayed a little longer and then parted at the gate.

'See you, Agnes.'

It seemed a bit odd, like a final goodbye rather than a see you tomorrow.

'Billy?'

He looked and smiled.

'See you tomorrow.' I smiled back.

CHAPTER 17

Attachment

I slept through. Awakened by the sound of Mum thumping the hoover against my door.

It was Saturday, why did she have to do that?

The clock raged 10.11am at me. Late. And my room felt chilly.

I pulled the covers in tighter and wandered around the room with my eyes. Something had happened but I'm not sure what. There were marks on the wall. Short, thin lines that didn't make a pattern, just a nest of sketches or scratches.

It wasn't real. I closed my eyes and pulled in tight. Saturdays were the longest as Mum was around and I had nowhere to go.

The day felt heavy with the thudding. Determined, I dressed quickly. I transferred the brooch to a t-shirt… a little crumpled but it was okay for a Saturday. The broach twinkled in the mirror.

Sometimes things are meant for us, even though we think they aren't.

The thudding of the hoover stopped. Maybe a distraction. Or she had made the stair carpet threadbare and we were through to floorboards. I opened my door, half expecting her to be stood there. Strangely, it was quiet.

I slipped down the stairs. Hoping to get out before a verbal questionnaire of my day's plans. I wasn't so lucky.

'Where you going?'

'To meet a friend,' I responded awkwardly. Lying was not my forte.

'A boyfriend?'

'I don't have a boyfriend Mum.'

'Not what I heard.'

The small-town workings were active!

'What d'you mean?'

'That weird thing from the shop. Can't iron his clothes. What are you doing being with him?'

I almost responded but felt it better to just leave. She had a look that would take me back up to my room and to sleep, or to drown in a bottle.

‘I’m going out.’

She was muttering but I pretended not to hear. I closed the door slowly behind me with a gentle click, put my hands in my pockets, and walked down the path. Not sure where I thought I was going but I was urged towards the corner shop.

It seemed busier today. People were urgently driving towards the town centre. Maybe in need of some retail therapy. Road works by the shop built up a queue. The odd impatient beep echoed along the road.

The door to the corner shop was open as usual, but no Billy today. I tentatively walked in, feeling like the only time I ever entered the shop, was for my usual but this time was different. Ravi, the owner, looked up and nodded his head. He was then distracted by a phone ringing. I lingered in the aisle wondering what I was actually doing. Starting to feel like I was being watched, I decided Billy must be out on an errand or something, so I left without buying anything – I had actually gone in there without buying vodka!

I headed up towards the bakery but then decided against cake also and veered off into the park. There weren’t too many people around. I looked around furtively before launching into a handstand.

After a few attempts it became clear that I wouldn't be doing it on my own for a while yet and needed Billy to help me a bit more. I decided to do a lap of the park before going back to the shop. Passing Bob's bench, I paused. Bob would have been here many times looking out at the park and the people walking by. Conversation, laughter and sadness. He would have witnessed it all.

Who was Bob? I hadn't asked the question. He must have had an interesting life. Maybe he had achieved great things? I mean, why else would somebody have a bench dedicated to them? Perhaps Hagrid would know? He seemed to be part of the furniture here also. Yes, I would ask him next time.

I returned back to the corner shop. This time sure that Billy would be leaning on the door, hands in pockets, grinning out at the world. I felt warm thinking about him.

This soon dissipated when I turned the corner and saw the empty doorway. I began to feel an internal gnawing. Just a small gurgling that something wasn't quite right.

As I entered the shop I could see Ravi was on the phone. I lingered. Unsure what to do next but with the need to know something ... to find Billy. And re-live yesterday again. The words of Ravi's conversation sought me out as I browsed the shelves.

'... yes... I know, it's okay though as I have somebody starting tomorrow.... Who Billy?.... no he left this morning... he's gone to London.... No he didn't want to come back... said he doesn't want to stay here.'

My heart fluttered. And my stomach dropped. Billy had gone?

The world around me filled up with a grey fog, clouding and reaching into every angle that I turned. I stumbled towards the door. Trying to inhale but making short gasps. Reaching for the door, the bollard, anything that would hold me. Tears flowed, effortlessly rolling as I staggered between the cars. Not looking. Not caring.

Why hadn't he told me? Why? I walked aimlessly. Finding myself back in the only place I felt I belonged and that welcomed me.

Was it all just a joke? A stupid, silly joke. To get me to do handstands in the park. Make a total fool of myself.

What are you doing with him? He's no good you know.

The words ricocheted in my head. Mum's then Tracey's. Repeat.

But… the brooch… why give me this? I ran my finger around the petals. No one would give a gift if they didn't like somebody.

But that means you think he liked you, Agnes. He went to all that trouble to meet me at the bakery. *Doesn't mean he liked you, maybe he was just passing time*. He held my arm when we walked and winked at me like…. *He does this to everybody, you're not special*. No. No, no, no.

I sat down on Bob's bench and sobbed. How had I let myself be duped into thinking I had a friend…a…boy…friend?

Had hours or minutes passed, I couldn't tell. And neither did I care. Except when the familiar stench caught me. Close by or just more unwashed – it was intense. I felt the warmth of a dirty hand touch my arm. I wasn't startled. I could smell Hagrid from 100 miles away. This kind gesture made my body heave with the pain.

He shuffled to make himself comfortable.

'Feels like a heart breaking.' He looked from under the fluffy untamed eyebrows and waited patiently.

Something about our growing friendship meant that we could have conversations without saying anything. Just those few words seemingly enough. And what could I say out loud anyway?

He held me with his fluffy eyebrow-lidded eyes as I melted in a sea of emotion. Allowing it to surround both of us until it dried up.

'I knew Bob. Used to call him the Ringmaster. Wouldn't catch him sitting on this bench though... oh no. He was out there taming the lions. Was a joker was Bob. Liked to entertain people. Never would hurt a flea. But he did know a thing or two about conjuring things up. Bit of a magician too.'

'A magician?' I questioned.

Hagrid nodded slowly. He leaned in closer to me, talking in lowered tones, 'Always believed that nothing you see around you is real... said it was all make believe.'

Hagrid nodded again and looked knowingly at me. 'It's secret Agnes.'

I looked expectantly. 'This bench isn't real?' I giggled. 'So, what are we sat on,' I asked. Equally wondering if I was going to drop on to the mud beneath with a thud.

'No… no… no…. it's not real,' he tapped the bench. 'It's a bench… but it's not a bench. Nothing is as it seems Agnes. Remember this when your heart is breaking lovely Agnes. Nothing is as it seems.'

Hagrid was so serious I couldn't bring myself to giggle further. The distraction was welcome. But it all came full circle back to Billy.

'What if Ravi had been talking about another Billy? I mean I shouldn't have been listening to somebody else's conversation anyway. I can go back and ask. I will go back and ask. And now I've just wasted your time. I mean…. .'

'Sometimes you just know though Agnes. Gotta trust this,' he tapped his chest.

My momentary light dimmed a bit.

'What do you mean?'

‘I dunno Agnes… but I know I gotta eat.’ A groan came from his tummy, or maybe it was a fart, and he smiled a hairy smile. Content with himself.

‘Trust your good self, Agnes’.

I stayed with Bob and the not real bench. I found myself exploring each petal of the brooch. And exploring my day. Flipping between light thoughts of being wrong and it was another Billy that Ravi talked about, to the darkness of no Billy being around. Had I asked? No.

I would go back. I would go back and ask. And then I would know for sure. That’s what I would do.

I took a deep breath and exhaled as I faced the shop from the across the road. No Billy.

CHAPTER 18

Derailed

I slugged from the bottle. Enjoying the burn. A familiar and joyful indication of bliss. I had every reason to enjoy this. I didn't need anything or anyone else to be around.

Each drink was followed by momentary reminiscence of the past couple of days. Followed by a drink. Followed by a tear or two. Followed by resentment.

Why hadn't he told me?

Gone Agnes. He was always going. Pain in the arse, he was. Never looked smart. And always busy doing handstands. Something a bit wrong there if you ask me.

I had spent half an hour sat on a chair listening to Ravi talk about his shop. But I wasn't really listening. In the end he gave me the bottle of vodka and sent me on my way with a request to make sure I didn't stress too much about Billy. There's plenty of nice boys in the town who would give their right little finger. Not sure whether that was a compliment or not. Why not a hand?

I sat on my bed allowing the numbness to flush over me. Feeling the pain but unsure of why. Just a few days of somebody showing me some attention. He had screwed up t-shirts anyway.

I felt myself relaxing into the bed, the space, the warmth.

There was a tapping. Familiar. Regular. I looked at the clock. 3.00am blared out at me. Always the same time. I noticed a box shape on the wall. Couldn't remember if I had put something there or not – given the sea of clothes. But it was illuminated somehow. I felt relaxed and sleepy but intrigued. The light outside reflected a multitude of images.

I closed my eyes again. Drifting.

A banging, parping and ringing took me by surprise. A band ringing out loud in my room. I sat up and scanned the room. Nothing but the box and the music.

Then a small shift of the box lid up and down to the tune. Puffing out a little smoke each time.

Lights twirled on the wall and the box opened fully in a plume of smoke. As this wavered and then started to melt into nothing I was confronted by a figure in a very tall top hat, tails and the shiniest boots. It was both grand and petrifying.

Head tilted down I couldn't see the face but the body was lithe and framed by the fitted, tailed jacket, on top of a crisp white shirt.

What disturbed me most was the fact that the figure leaned on a stick attached to a very long whip.

My mind circled back to the conversation with Hagrid and his reminder of Bob the …… oh my God… the Ringmaster.

It was all coming to me now. Was this him?

Very slowly the hat lifted exposing the face. Clear white skin, dark eyes, and very red lips.

'Bob?' It came out before I had any control over it. Or maybe I didn't. And now I was exposed.

The lips parted in a small smile. But the eyes. They glittered.

The following was something that I only saw once. I only needed to see it once.

I watched on as Bob stepped out of the box. At a tap it crumbled into ashes then twirled in a circle at the response of the whip. An energy that swirled, grew, and titillated each and every part of the wall. Clearing the tree, the branches, and all the images that the streetlight and moon illuminated.

There was a moment of intense stillness. A child entered and sat on the skirting and watched. Bob straightened, his whole torso stretched up, increasing his presence. Followed by a crack as his whip snaked rapidly through the air.

A lion stepped in. A fluffy mane framing the beautiful features of its face as it gracefully paced and sniffed around the room. Stepping in and out of the clothes. The sharp crack stopped all movement. The lion's nostrils flaring as it waited. The whip cracked and the lion went up on its back legs, padding on large rear paws, then leaped between spaces, laid down and proceeded to waggle its pads like a baby. 'Aws,' and 'Ahs,' were loud from the audience. The spectacle ended as the lion righted itself, wandered and diminished into the wall and a leafy jungle.

Bob stood still, head lowered, but his eyes seeking forward. A crescendo of music crowned the room as a clown entered. Full of spirit and fun. Acrobatics gone wrong with a sad face. Plates balanced with a sense of pride. A unicycle round and round and round the ring. And cake pies smashed into his own face.

A sharp slash filled the air again. Stopping the music, the air, sound and light. The child shrunk back. I pulled up the duvet, not sure. Holding my breath.

Stillness hung. Silence pierced. Steps echoed.

As if in an auditorium. Bob came to the centre of the ring bringing the clown with him, wide eyed.

Bob whispered in the clown's ear.

A gentle vibration of music filled the air with warmth, intention and a feeling of goodness.

The clown stood. Bathed in a single light he started to peel off layer upon layer of clothing, make up, expressions, until everything had been removed. A person stood before me who was familiar. Their outline solid and their centre bathed in and exuding light.

The child looked up from their seat, smiled and held out arms. I too looked up and smiled.

Billy.

We all watched as he turned and walked into the whiteness. Jauntily moving amongst soft tones of warm light as he very slowly disappeared, becoming a very distant dot. And then nothing.

I wept. Both in joy and in sadness.

The loud parp of my alarm woke me. 6.00am. I panicked and started to pull on clothes with a heavy head and heart. Did I really have to work today? I could see the small remnants in the bottle, taunting me. Calling for another round.

As I scuffled trying to find some uncreased clothes I came across the brooch. I sat down on my bed and held it tightly.

Some things are just meant for us even though we think they aren't.

As I slowly trod the stairs and was met with Mum in her dressing gown.

'Bit early for a Sunday Agnes. You ok?'

'Sunday?' I felt life drain from me.

'You need to iron that top before you go out anywhere.'

I remounted the stairs and climbed into bed – t-shirt was screwed up anyway.

CHAPTER 19

Visiting hour

Dearest loveliest Agnes

I visited you in your dream. I hope you saw me. It's all the circus of life my dear. Doing what is expected of us so as not to be judged. Then we get a little bit of light come in and oh.. my …the joy it is beyond stupendous. Just something to give you a gentle nudge in the right direction.

What you learn through others is pulling you towards the light my dear. That most magical rainbow of beautiful light that you can't help but want to take a peek at. It's there Agnes.

Don't forget to take another look. Satnav says do a u-turn. Look for the signs. We are EVERYWHERE!

Say hi to H for me.

I'm skipping with sparkles.. you are doing so well.

Toodaloo!

My most, biggest love and starry hugs

Bob

x

CHAPTER 20

Seeing as you are

The days passed, leaving a trail of nothingness behind them. The dreams came and went with the circus being a recurring theme.

Tracey seemed happier than ever. I had tucked back into my habits of nightly drinking. Quietly making it through the day until the next opportunity to meet with my reliable bottle of Russian Pride. The only reason I worked, was so that I would have the money to buy it and not borrow.

On the Wednesday evening it was a particularly sunny day. The heat tired me, so I took a slow meander home. As I came closer to the corner shop my heart pulsated. Somebody was leaning in the doorway. Just how Billy used to. Was it him? I got closer and could see that the figure was well dressed. Ironed clothes, but some similarities in the way that he stood.

'Excuse me.' I whispered. He moved instinctively as though he had only just seen me, despite my closeness. I scuttled to the back of the shop and self-consciously grabbed a bottle and hid it under my arm before taking it to the counter. Ravi carried on his conversation with the man in the doorway. I waited patiently, hoping I was invisible enough but not so much that he didn't notice me.

'He's happy – working with the homeless – or something like that with a charity.' The man spoke confidently.

'Oh good, much better suited to him than something like this... he was always talking to people rather than working...... ah Agnes... ' he took the bottle and scanned it, put it in a bag and took my money.

'Had a bit of a soft spot for Agnes, I think.' I looked at Ravi, mortified that he was bringing me in to the conversation.

'Oh, so you're Agnes, are you?' I looked at the man, the familiarity of his features distracting. He winked.

My face lit with the heat of fire.

'I um, I ... you... know Billy?'

'I'm his brother.' He tilted his head slightly and looked at me, smiling. 'He talked about you when I spoke to him yesterday. In fact, he said something about a daisy, but I have no idea what he was going on about. Said he would catch up with you one day.'

I nodded, in hope and recognition. I needed to escape or I would melt but I also wanted to laugh and cry in equal measure. He still remembered me. I muttered a 'bye' as I left the shop at rapid speed.

Instead of heading home, I found myself in the park. Watching people lay in the sun, children running around and dogs fetching balls. I walked with no intention but came to a stop near Bob's bench. It wasn't free today.

An old lady sat. A light pink hat with a curled rim propped on her small head. Her sunken eyes glared through me and whilst there was still space, I felt as though I was intruding. I sat down on the grass a short distance away and allowed the sun to melt away the remainder of the adrenaline coursing round my body.

Billy had mentioned me to his brother. And also the daisy? The daisy. What had I done with it? I rooted around in my pockets, back ones, front ones, jeans, jacket. It wasn't there. Then a gentle dig in the chest reminded me I had attached it to my t shirt. I unclipped it.

I gripped it tightly and held my face up to the sun. Just like a flower I thought. Always turning to face the light. I allowed the warmth to wash over me fully. Letting go. The birds sung loudly and children laughed in joy. I didn't often hear these sounds, usually the harsher noises took over.

My momentary bliss was interrupted.

'Get away from me you smelly beast. You can't sit there. You mustn't have had a bath in years. Can you smell yourself? Terrible. Absolutely terrible.'

I peeked out of one eye to see Hagrid stood, looking a little awkward. Unused to such a response to his presence he looked almost childlike.

'Don't stand there looking like a child. You're a grown man, you should know better. You can't possibly stay here a moment longer. Shooo before I scream.'

Hagrid shuffled off a few feet. Glanced back and then continued.

I grabbed my bags and walked quickly after him.

'Hagrid.'

He stopped.

'It's not Hagrid.' A hint of annoyance surrounded the words.

‘What’s not?’ I asked cautiously.

‘Me name.’

‘I know…. I know… I mean..it just… suits you….. What is your real name?’

He looked suspiciously at me.

‘What you want to know for?’

I didn’t. I didn’t need to know. But now I felt like I wanted to.

‘It would be nice to know your name.’

‘Schubert.’ He grumbled.

‘Sherbet?’

‘Just call me Hagrid.’

‘No.. no …. If Sherbet’s your name then I should call you that.’ I offered trying to lighten his irritation.

He turned to look at me and laughed.

‘I think she’d prefer I smell of sherbet,’ he gestured towards the lady.

We laughed. ‘Schubert was me dad’s name.’

It was the first time he had mentioned family. We walked in silence. Me imagining another version called Schubert and Hagrid looking like he was slowly coming back to Hagrid. 'You're a good person Agnes.' This was followed by more silence. 'You still sad?'

I wasn't sure how to answer this. *Was I sad?*

'No, not really... but what's there to be happy about?'

He stopped and looked at me. I wasn't sure if there was a lecture in there somewhere or if he was lost for words. I followed his view as he looked around the park. Then we continued to walk heading back to the bench.

'I don't think I smell Agnes... do you? ... it's people smelling themselves... they's rotting from the insides.'

I quite liked that. Though I did get the odd whiff of the intrusive odour. Perhaps it did say more about me than it did about him.

We did another circuit of the park without talk of Billy. Just about smells, trees and the ability to hear nature when the noise of life was barking so loudly.

As we came back past the bench it was empty.

‘I wonder what Bob was like. How did you know him?’

‘Bob didn’t believe in the ordinary way. He saw things as they was. Natural like.’

‘He said …’ there was a drawn out space as I hung on, ‘…we was all part of some special plan but most don’t see it. You sees it from the space where you are. Like if it’s not a good space. But then sometimes it’s a good space even when it’s not a good space cause it means you have been there.’

We allowed silence after this. It was a long speech for Hagrid. I didn’t think I had heard him say so much in one go before. And I think I understood. A little.

The sun started to make its way down and Hagrid said he had to go for his dinner.

‘You go home too Agnes. You don’t need that stuff.’ He pointed to my carrier bag. And off he shuffled.

He was right, of course, I didn’t need it. And, usually, I wanted it, but not tonight.

CHAPTER 21

Repeat

I walked slowly home considering Hagrid. 'It's people smelling themselves.... They're rotten from the insides out.' Maybe it was true. I liked Hagrid. But I could smell him.... It wasn't good at all.

I pulled my t-shirt up and sniffed it. Just to check.

The double lock was on so Mum was out somewhere. Unusual for her but we hadn't really spoken. I breathed rather than tensing my way into the house.

Taking my time I went to the kitchen for a drink of water – keeping Hagrid's advice in mind. As I went to leave, I noticed a note on the table.

'Gone out for dinner. There's soup in the fridge.'

I stood watching the garden grow, wondering who she might have gone out with. She had probably stood here doing the same. A little of which didn't sit well, as that would mean I was like her. Or was that just what we were all like?

The garden was clear, plants and flowers just so, and the bird bath placed exactly in the centre. I was as far from this as the

Sahara Desert to the North Pole. It made me feel less like being exact. And the need not to tidy my room.

I made some cheese on toast and sat in the kitchen to eat. Feeling some sort of liberation that nobody was going to appear and tell me what to put here or there or question my choice of dinner.

The birds flew in and out. Their business delaying the time before I went to my room. Even as dusk set in and eventually darkness, I didn't want to the turn the lights on. The silence was like a warm relaxing bath. I was dozing and slow to move. The mild sounds, in the background, of the key in the door and footsteps, didn't register.

The light went on and Mum stood looking fiercely.

'What on earth are you doing sat here in the dark you silly girl? You frightened the life out of me. You are odd sometimes.' She was edgy.

'Did you have a nice dinner?' I questioned, wanting her to respond with the details of a man friend. Would that be possible? Was there a man who would suit my mum? Or one that my mum would suit was maybe the question.

'It was very nice.' She rooted around in the fridge. 'Looks like you didn't have the soup. Oh Agnes, you have to eat. Did you have anything yet?'

I stood up and ran the water in the sink and washed my plate.

'Well ... what did you have?'

'Toast with cheese.' Why not cheese on toast I didn't know but it seemed better, more tasteful.

'Well, that's not enough is it. You need to eat more healthily. You should have some cooking lessons - that would be helpful. Then when you find yourself another good man, you can do the cooking and things you should have been able to do with Dan.'

This was like another onslaught of arrows. My shoulders bristled. The atmosphere changed. I gripped the carrier bag from the table, walked from the kitchen without a word and went to my room.

I drank straight from the bottle and felt the delicious burn.

Layer after layer of the liquid allowed me to shift deeper and deeper into the numbness. As I started to drift, I remembered Hagrid's words. And I wondered if it was the same for Mum.

She didn’t much like that I hadn’t been able to keep Dan happy. Was I really such a disappointment? Or was the disappointment about her own inability to keep somebody happy?

I went into sleep troubled. But slept, nonetheless.

CHAPTER 22

Old patterns

I woke heavily. The clock blared a very red 8.22am at me.

I moved with a speed that was not uncommon to a deer getting out of danger. This was not good. I was late. And Tracey was in today. What, what, what could I say?

I cleaned my teeth, but that was about it. Dressed in yesterday's clothes. Broach pinned. I ran down the stairs and out into the street. At the end of the road, I had to stop to catch my breath. I should have listened to Hagrid.

At the shop window I could see Tracey serving a customer. She looked towards me with no expression and continued. I felt the sharp, spiky energy as I passed behind her.

Ruth was looking flushed.

'Where you been?' She whispered. 'She's been going mad... thought she was going to blow a fuse.'

'I overslept Ruth.... I know it's bad but I just..... I think I need the toi......' I rushed into the toilet and emptied the contents of my stomach. I repeated until there was nothing left.

I could hear mumbled conversation as I sat waiting for another bout. At least I could say I was ill. Not that it was self-inflicted of course.

Tracey's tones pierced the door. 'Agnes. I want you out of there and out of the shop. Can't have the customers hearing this. Best this doesn't happen again. Last warning.'

I quivered a little. A coldness had spread through my body. I couldn't do this again.

Gentle tones came through the door. 'Ag… it's me… you ok? She's just popped across the road to the pharmacy, you can come out.' I emerged sheepishly. 'Oh gal, you look terrible. Did you eat something?' I loved Ruth. She was just kindness all the way through. Even if she knew it wasn't the truth.

'Yes, must've done. Had a curry last night.'

'Go on. Best get yourself home and rest. Let me know if you can't do tomorrow as it's just me and you.' Her attempt at a wink was dramatic with both eyes shut.

I was just coming out of the shop as Tracey came in. She didn't look at me or say anything.

Something shifted and I felt the urge to speak. 'Tracey?'

She turned to look, surprised.

'I have to go home as I've been unwell, as you know. I will be in tomorrow. This will never happen again.'

She nodded. I felt her watch me go off down the road.

At that precise moment, I knew that I would not spend the rest of my life working in the bakers. I couldn't. But there were lots of other things I couldn't do either.

The journey home was as quick as the one there. As I reached the garden gate Mum was just leaving the house. My timing seemed to be impeccable today.

'What you doing back? You look awful - did something happen?'

'Just running and forgot something. See you later.'

'Alright…. Well… ' and off she went.

I flopped onto my bed, lay arms out and stared up at the ceiling. Thoughts abundant but none that were helpful it seemed, as they all led to the same idea of drink and that this wasn't working. Was it?

The floor was dressed with discarded clothes, dresser clogged with bits of paper and books, make up, hair products... all that I had since leaving Dan. I was a mess. My hair smelled of sick. I was rotting from the inside out.... Hagrid was right.

I spent the morning drinking water. Making the floor look like the floor. Throwing away anything I didn't need. Letting air in the room. I stuck my head out of the window and enjoyed a moment of fresh, gentle breeze pouring into my face.

Room clear. Head slightly fuzzy but clearer. I laid down on the bed that I had just made properly. It felt like I was being enveloped in a soft warm cloak. Filling me up with a sense of peace. The sun filtered through the window glass and open space. The air littered with tiny particles of fluff that circled slowly and then with more speed when a breeze came in.

I felt myself drifting.

CHAPTER 23

Always with you

A gentle 'ssssshhhhhh,' echoed around the room.

Bob sat at the end of the bed. Legs crossed. Jiggling a leg. Watching Agnes. Switching legs and jiggling the other. A brief pause and then unfolding his legs.

A rustle echoed round the room as he stood. Eyes moving left, then right.

Agnes continued to sleep.

He moved closer to her side and looked on lovingly. Stroking her hair without touching. Tender.

In quiet child-like tones he began ... 'Shall I tell you a story darling Agnes? It is such a delight.' He giggled and rubbed his hands together.

'This is the tale of a little girl who is stuck in a space. Not just any space... in fact, it could be outer space for all we know as it was in mid-air and very, very dark. But there were no doors or windows. Hmmmm....,' a confused look.

'Yes, *no* doors, *no* windows. And it felt as *tight* as a corset in this space where nothing else existed. and she was so, so, very lonely.' For a moment Bob looked concerned and thoughtful. Then a smile broadened.

'But there were others in this space, you see Agnes, there were others with her. They had been there alllll along. Strangely.... or not....depending on how you see it..... they weren't uncomfortable. You see, its darkness was a comfort, it felt safe to them. Can you imagine?' He looked at Agnes with a questioning look. Waiting for a response it seemed.

'Rather excitingly, once in a blue moon, there would be a flash of light. This would cause such a hullaballoo of excitement as they could see each other and lots of other things as well. They would oooooo and aaaaahhhh.' He glanced, waiting. 'Exciting, yes?'

'Well, this little girl really fell in love with what she could see in the flashes but would only keep her eyes open for a smidge of a second. Like this,' he blinked rapidly.

'And over lots of flashes she began to keep her eyes open longer and longer.' He used his thumb and index finger to open his eyes. 'Ha, fishbowl eyes Agnes.' His laughter gently caressed the room.

'There was more out there in those little corners you see. When everyone was looking at the flashes and the very strange things appearing in front of them, the little girl looked behind and everywhere else and saw that where the light came from, there was a lot of very lovely other colours too.' His hands starting to move in a wilder fashion.

'She desperately wanted to explore. Like a brave warrior.' His chest puffed out and hands came to his hips. He strutted round the room with bravado. Stopping back at the bed, he looked closely at Agnes with the expression of a mother meeting her new born.

'Agnes darling, it's a bit like only focusing on the one moon and being too scared to look anywhere else because that lovely, beautiful moon means everything to you even though it isn't giving you anything back. Oh sweetest, loveliest one.... look away from that moon. Look away and see all that sparkles just right behind it, around it... around you. And trust.'

Bob sat and stared for some time as Agnes mumbled in her sleep. Tranquil, yet troubled.

'Time to go now sweetie. Toodeloo for now.' He blew a kiss and took long strides across the clear floor, did a perfect cartwheel, and swept his hands up high above his head as if to take off. He smiled and winked.

A gentle breeze blew in through the window.

Bob hovered as Agnes woke. Gnawing and licking her lips she sat up on her elbows. Her eyes searching the room and watching a feather floating down. It settled gently on the carpet.

The windows shared the grumbling clouds and the hint of rain as small droplets landed on the pane. Small, dainty, and ineffective at first. Then the storm came, clearing everything.

CHAPTER 24

Connecting to the light

It was Friday. I arrived early to work and set up trays, cakes and breads meticulously.

'Glad you came in today Ags. Was worried you wouldn't,' Ruth giggled and shrugged her shoulders up – a lovable trait. 'You want to go to the market when we finish? There's a new one up Moon Street.'

'Err, I don't have much money but... yes,' I was surprised at her offer and my response. And also that there was something outside of my home, the bakery and the park. Somewhere new.

I worked harder than I normally did despite there being nobody to show. No Tracey to be in line with. Just me and the customers who seemed to linger longer. Creating a queue, but adding to the good feeling of the day.

A small part of me expected to look up to see a crumpled t-shirt and a smiling Billy. I wondered what he was doing at that moment. Maybe he would come back. Perhaps Ravi was wrong. I pondered the idea before I was distracted by a 'You aren't coming in here you smelly old thing.... get gone with you.' I looked up to see Hagrid stood at the window. He waved and looked longingly at the cakes.

'Bear with me a second,' I asked the customer. I took an ice cream cone cake and went to the shop door and gave it to Hagrid. He smiled a beardy smile and wondered off gently holding his cake.

Nobody uttered a word except the lady who had shooed him away. 'Well! That's not the thing to do. Shouldn't be encouraging him. Imagine all of those nasties.' I put on a new pair of gloves to serve her and she went away happy.

We cleared quickly, but efficiently, so Tracey had no complaints on Saturday morning and then we left together, excited.

I wasn't sure I had ever ventured left out of the shop. Or it didn't feel like I had. Everything seemed new, though I had grown up here, so it was the new old.

We walked slowly and talked. I think it was the only time I had seen Ruth without food in her mouth. I noticed her breathing becoming louder as we sped up a little and so slowed down until she was okay.

'I need to stop eating them cakes Ags,' she grinned and raised her shoulders. 'We're nearly there though. You're gonna love it.'

We took a final turn and I saw the street sign. We were in Moon Street. There were, what seemed like, a sea of market stalls all the way into the horizon, each selling different things - or should I say different versions of the same things. The fruit stalls had the most beautiful array of colours. The clothes danced in the breeze and the jewellery sparkled in the sun. Plus, a book stall of second hand or used but new.

I lingered and ran my fingers across the books. Endless subjects. Ruth stood and waited impatiently. I hadn't read in some time and felt strangely hungry to start again. Whilst I was trailing my eyes over all the titles the stall holder returned.

He looked on. Arms crossed. Pondering.

'Something in particular?' came out suddenly but gently.

'No... err.... No.....I just like books.'

'Me too.' The silence in between seemed to bring everything else around to a standstill. I was beginning to feel uncomfortable with the intense feeling that I was being watched carefully. The pressure of this caused me to move away. As I moved, I looked up straight into light blue pools. The eyes were odd and yet familiar.

'I wonder if you might like this?' He offered me a slightly battered cream coloured book with the word 'inward' implanted in what looked like a red stamp mark. My eyes returned to his. 'It's a wonderful book if you're looking for something.'

I looked away at Ruth. I didn't have much money now and didn't want to waste what I had. Shaking my head, I left the stall.

Ruth was stood behind me and giggled. 'I think he wanted you to have that.'

'There are so many beautiful things here I don't want to waste my money on a book.' Beautiful things. I touched my brooch. This was beautiful to me.

'It was probably about innies and outies ….,' Ruth offered grinning. Then looked at me and quietly but honestly stated. 'I think you're beautiful and you don't see it.'

I laughed and steered her to the next brightly coloured jewellery store where her eyes lit up. It seemed we had found

Ruth's passion. We spent the next hour trying necklaces on her and being unable to decide which was her favourite. She ended up choosing a moon-shaped pendant on a long chain. The moon element seemed rather surreal given the name of the street. We joked about howling our way home like werewolves and made our way slowly back along the market stalls towards home.

We ambled passed the book stall again, or where it had been. There was just a bench remaining. Gone already.

I wondered what the book was that he had shown me. Inwards and upwards is all I could think -which I shared with Ruth. We literally howled with laughter all the way to the end of the street, then went our separate ways.

As I laid thinking about the day, I just remembered the book stall. Nothing else. 'Inwards,' I said out loud. And laughed at Ruth's joke about belly buttons. The day was one of the best I had had in a while. Friday, in a market, on Moon Street. Who'd have thought?

The veils of sleep started to gently drift over me. The clock shone brightly at 11:11pm as I succumbed.

Chapter 25

The light

'Roll up, roll up. Get your tickets for the greatest spectacular, the fantabulous, the one, the only.... Ringmaster Extraordinaire. This is the most magical show you will ever see. Just one ticket left.'

The clown came towards me holding out the ticket.

'Surely you cannot miss out on this one Miss. Would you like this ticket?'

Unable to speak, though my mouth moved, I took the ticket.

The atmosphere was zipping with crackles of electricity. A man on stilts walked by, though his legs were incredibly long his arms were too. Hands made of flowers. As if I saw this everyday, I waved at him. Happy to see that he had arms as long as me. Mine reached the end of the bed almost touching my ankles.

'All of the tickets are now sold, ladies and gentlemen.' There were groans of disappointment.

'But don't despair, this will all be happening again soon. This will be repeated so you can all see this amazing magic. Again, and again.'

Roars of happiness echoed all around. Peculiar in that I couldn't see these people but it felt joyful nonetheless.

The tall man came to stand near me and smiled. He reached his flower hand down for mine. As I lifted my arm and extended my hand, I saw that I too had flower hands. Daisies.

We walked hand in hand into the circus tent.

I took a seat right at the front. The trapeze swung as though somebody were on it, balls circled in the air as if they were being juggled, an elephant marched like a band leader holding a baton with its trunk. And I sat with my fellow invisible audience members.

The tall man disappeared back out of the tent. As he did, everything stopped in motion. The balls hung magically in the air, perfectly positioned. The trapeze held in time in forward motion. The elephant stood with one foot up and the baton high as if a crescendo had been reached. I turned to see a rather desolate sea of chairs. And then the other way all empty. I was alone.

I stood and gathered my arms. Folding them around my daisies like little posies. Every step I took felt weightless and I had a sense I was somewhere like the moon… only not. I stepped into the ring and walked slowly towards the elephant. I had never seen one close up before. What a sight to behold. I ran my flowery hands over the deep crevices that were the lines of beauty on this magnificent creature. Leg still raised the elephant was sturdy, although precariously balanced.

'A true wonder, yes?' I startled at the sound.

A very pale man stood before me dressed in a tall black hat, red tails, and black high boots.

Eyes widening he spoke again, 'I said… a true wonder.' He came close to my face looking. Searching.

I tried to speak but couldn't. Nothing come out just endless mouth movements.

'Ah, yes, I forgot, doesn't matter.' He muttered and then stood for a moment contemplating the roof of the tent. And then looking back at me. He must have repeated this movement about ten times but all I could do was wait.

He paced forward four paces, turned and took four paces and again and again, making a square. 'There... I think we are ready. I think you are ready. Just step back a little.'

Taking the baton from the elephant he waved it in the air, whispering random words that didn't make any sense. As soon as he stopped, a grinding noise appeared from above. A bit like stone on stone. As it started getting louder, a light channelled its way down to the centre of the ring. And as the noise continued the light became wider and filled the space... a square marked out in the centre of the ring.

The light was clear white at first but then it started to fade, becoming mixed in with other colours, intense, radiant, and also some gentle pastels.

I felt myself being effortlessly moved towards this light and colour. Being guided towards the doorway that appeared in a slim shape. As I got closer, the door opened and the light gushed out. It was so intense I had to cover my eyes from the pain. Again, I tried to open them but couldn't.

'Wait to adjust,' a voice whispered from behind. But how long was the wait? And then I knew, as I covered my eyes with my daisy hands the petals caught the glare. Deflecting it. And allowing me to see. The beauty of what I could see was indescribable. The power of the feeling of love multiplied over and over. Could it be real? The textures, sounds and smells of all before me were overwhelming but they caressed me so well I couldn't look away.

I moved further in. Sniffing in the scents of something new. That I had no experience of and yes, like seeing through the eyes of the newborn child. Wild and free but with a safety that comes from a mind that hasn't been intruded upon. How was this possible? How was I here? I turned to look back behind me. To find my guide. The man in the hat and red tails stood at some distance waving. Not frantically though. A jolly wave. I started to move back towards him and the entrance. It suddenly struck me that this was a foreign place, that I wasn't from here, so how did I get back? Was the door there? Where was the door? Why couldn't I see it? I pulled down my hands but the light was too much so I ran blindly in the direction from which I had come, hoping that I would run into the door and to the circus tent. I was struggling to breathe. What if there was no air? And I so needed the toilet. Was there a toilet?

Gasping for air I woke. Sweating. Heart racing. I visually searched my room, looking for signs of where I had been. Something. But all around me was clear. The floors were clear. My dresser clear. The window open wider than I had ever managed it before and the sun beaming in low.

'Agnes, you okay?' Mum's head popped round the door.

'Yes…. I… I think I was dreaming.'

'You were making a lot of noise. Just thought I would check.'

I listened to her steps going down the stairs. Clanging pots and pans in the kitchen. Her weekly tidy up. Everything in its place.

CHAPTER 26

The note

I left the house for a walk. Troubled by my dream though I couldn't remember it all. It felt like I had been abducted by aliens. I laughed to myself at the ridiculousness. What was the whole circus thing about anyway?

As I passed the corner shop the door was open, but nobody stood in it. I wandered past. Aimless really, as I didn't have a plan but couldn't sit in the house. My thoughts returned to Billy and I wondered if he thought of me much.

I reached for my brooch but found a space instead. I stopped in the middle of the pavement. Somebody behind me had to do a last minute swerve. 'What you doing?' a touch of annoyance filtered through.

'I'm sorry, I er..,' I muttered, quietly, explaining that I had forgotten my brooch. I felt odd without it and uncomfortable. Weighing up whether to go back home and get it or not, my thoughts were interrupted.

'Agnes. What are you doing just standing there?' Mum's dulcet tones drilled in. I turned to face her.

‘I forgot something.’ The annoyance in my voice was evident.

‘Well it’s a bit of a bloody silly place to stop.’

‘I know, it just…………,’ I was about to explain but I realised that it would reach little understanding and so I diverted the conversation.

‘Where are you going to?’

‘I’m popping up to the bakery and then to the market.’

‘The market?’

‘Yes dear, the one on Moon Street.’

‘Oh, well, have a nice time.’ I was surprised. Markets weren’t Mum’s thing and definitely not the one on Moon Street.

I watched her walk on and felt the urge to follow her. Perhaps she hadn’t been before. As she reached the bakery I could see her standing at the doorway. Then Tracey appeared. They wandered off together – chatting animatedly. Even laughing. Mum was laughing.

As soon as they turned into Moon Street I quickened my step, still unsure about what I was hoping to see. Perhaps Mum being so taken by all the beautiful colours and jewellery, the vibrant fruits, or even a book?

Turning into the market I was confronted with something very different than yesterday. The stalls were small, some with clothing that all seemed to be quite dull – whites, blacks, browns, dark red, blues. The fruit and vegetable stalls were dusty with offerings of vegetables pulled straight from the ground, left to sit for some time and starting to wrinkle.

Was this the same street?

I walked slowly and watched as people quite miserably served the few customers. Up ahead I could see Mum and Tracey talking and laughing still. Quite happy as they brought a few items. As I reached halfway along the street I could see the book stall a few stands up. This was the only stall that had colour that day. The very tall seller stood flicking through a book. As I came closer it was clear that the books were very much the same as yesterday. Brightly coloured bindings shining and sparkling. I went closer to the stand. Conscious that I might get caught here as Mum and Tracey made their return back along the street.

I stood looking at the books, running my fingers over them.

‘What do you like to read?’ the tall man spoke gently. I looked up into the light blue pools.

‘Um, anything really. I haven’t had much time recently though.’

‘What about this one? It’s a favourite of mine. Can’t go wrong with it.’ He offered the book from yesterday.

‘I, err, I don’t have any money with me today. I will keep it in mind.’ I looked away – feeling his stare and wondering if he had guessed it was a lie.

He offered the book again. ‘On me.’

I looked up. He looked even taller on closer inspection and was wearing gloves with a flowery pattern on them. I took the book from his outstretched hand. ‘Thank you.’

As I went to turn away, I heard Mum’s voice, ‘Well I’m surprised she’s managed to keep the job at all if I’m honest. I wasn’t aware of how she was though. And as for that boy well…’ I lost the rest as they walked past without any recognition. Almost like I wasn’t there. Or the book stall.

I stayed facing the counter until they were far enough along. The stall tender viewed me with a bemused look.

'I think you're safe now.' He chuckled and moved on to serve an impatient man who was rifling through the books and not caring where they landed.

I took a slow walk back up Moon Street, the dull colours uninspiring. People milling and looking downwards, not really acknowledging anything. And yet the book that I held was somehow like a sparkly rainbow. The slightly worn edges gave it an added layer of curiosity. It wasn't perfect. But that was perfect in itself. I pondered the thought.

As I walked back along the road, I passed the bakery on the other side of the road. I could see Tracey behind the counter. Constantly moving things around or tidying. The usual suspects hovering around the doorway, waiting to see if there would be any free cakes since it was almost closing time.

Maybe more today as Ruth wasn't in. I smiled at the thought of her.

When I got back home Mum was already in. Back in the kitchen. I went in to make a sandwich.

'Post for you,' she motioned towards the table.

There was no surname just 'Agnes' and the address in scrawly writing. As I picked it up the back curled up. It had been opened but I was more intrigued to find out who had written to me.

Mum was looking at me waiting.

The paper was crumpled and I didn't read the short letter at first, just looked to the bottom of the page. I could just make out Billy's name with a daisy by it. I felt a charge of warmth whip through me. The feeling unknown but known. Taking in a deep breath I devoured the contents.

'Hey Agnes, I'm sending this all the way from London. Ha! Got a job up here. Hope you haven't got all mopey cause you haven't seen my wrinkled t-shirt! Ha again! Keep going and keep up that handstand practice... oh and don't lose that daisy you stole. It was meant for you Ag, you know that. I will be seeing you in London soon. Love Billy'.

I didn't wait to hear what she had to say. I scuttled up to my room and read it five more times and then sat down and cried.

She never mentioned the letter though I knew she had read it. Made some assumptions from it no doubt; and she did somehow change from that day. There was more distance. She didn't bother me so much. It was like a release from something; perhaps more of me from her than the other way around. Or perhaps she had given up hope of making me how she wanted? Or of me getting back with Dan, somebody who was more perfect.

I read that letter every day. Short though it was it made me feel alight somehow. There was something more out there. Another world. Something more than Purbrey. And the bakery.

CHAPTER 27

The Invite

When I opened the book, a waft of oldness flew out and hit my nostrils. The pages were off colour to match. The hard cover was inset with gold script 'The Invite' and further down 'a tale of another world intertwined with this one' and then 'A M Love.'

When I opened it up further a piece of paper fluttered out.

'The best preparation for the future, is to live as if there were none' was written in flowing handwriting, signed off by B.

My hands tingled a little as I held the paper. It was an odd feeling. Like a pressure, or somebody or something, running their fingers over my fingers and palms. Tickling but with a barrier almost.

Was there something on my hands? I looked to see. Nothing.

I opened further pages and flicked through. But the quote in my hand was more... loud.

I laid back on my bed. I didn't really think about the future. Did I? Maybe I did. Thinking beyond the bakery is thinking of the future. It's impossible not to think of the future. What's tomorrow even? No Tracey tomorrow. So there... I thought about it. I needed to prepare. I needed to get myself out of Purbrey before I end up like... like...Mum. I don't want to be stuck here for the rest my life.

I flicked over the pages until I came to 'Beginning.' Not Chapter 1, it didn't seem to have them.

And then I read. And read. The sun went down. The night came in. And I read more.

CHAPTER 28

Stepping out

Darling Agnes

Oh, I am so excited to see you are reading 'The Invite.' To fall asleep in the middle of it is a magical dream. I can see we are going places now.

Did you know that I was there today watching you in the market? I was at the book stall just for a nanosecond. So it might be that you didn't get a glimpse of me.

Can you see that you have now stepped in to the light my dear? It's such a wonderful, glorious place especially when you can see the dark and the light. Because they cannot exist without one another. Not light without dark nor dark without light. It's this way, and that way, together.

I have a favourite ball that has a beautiful swirl carving through the middle like a wave. It's a yin yang. Bit like a yoyo.

In fact.... I've got one here. Oh, I love a yoyo.

The air whirred as the yoyo flew down and up, winding with its string. Agnes shifted.

Whoops, I think I might have stirred you from your dream.

I had better dash.

My lovely one... I'm with you always.

Lots of sparkles

Bob

Chapter 29

Practice

A thud roused me. I could see the bat hanging in his spot. The circus tent already in place with its flag flying jubilantly at the top of the tent.

I looked around the room to see if there was anybody else. Just one person stood outside the tent. A girl with a very jolly round happy face. She held three coloured balls in her hands. One purple, one blue, one green. She looked in my direction and smiled, and then started to juggle the balls in a very small circle. First it was just two balls, the purple and blue. Effortlessly spinning. Before the green entered without a stop. The girl smiled as she watched the balls go round and round. Then her attention came to me.

'Come and have a go Agnes! Come on. It's fun, and it really makes you feel like you're one of the balls.' She let out a short giggle. A familiar sound but I wasn't sure from where.

I had never been good at juggling. Mum would snatch the balls off me and roll her eyes as I failed again and again. I shook my head.

‘Come on,’ she urged. Still smiling. I think we can get you doing five. Wouldn’t that be something!’

She stepped forward and held out a hand that I couldn’t refuse. A plump, friendly hand that meant no harm.

‘Here’s two. Throw one up, pass the other one between your hands and catch it when it comes back down.’

I did as she said, slowly. It worked, but not in the circular way that she had worked with hers.

‘It’s not the same,’ I said despondently.

‘It is Ags, it is. Look, have another one. Throw it up and when it’s up there throw another and catch the one coming down, but throw the other one up when the third one is up here.’ She held her hand high.

I looked at the balls in my hands and back at her. Confused.

‘Here. I’ll show you.’ In seeming slow motion but still keeping the circle, she tossed a ball up… as it hung in the air and started its descent, she threw another and caught the one coming down and let the third follow the second up. As I watched the slow motion play it became clearer.

I took the balls and started. After dropping one I followed her actions. My oval turned and leaned. First one way and then the other. Gradually it began to even out. Until it became a perfect circle. Spinning in time with the girl's circle, I kept my focus directly at the centre. This is where it all seemed to be held together. Right there. Not in my hands, or at the balls. Not to the left, right or up to where the ball hovered before it began its descent. But right in the middle. It made the whole process much easier, effortless and simple.

'There you go Ags, you're amazing! No point in looking anywhere else is there? Just keep looking at the centre, right in front of you. That's all you need.'

She winked and then was gone into the tent.

I stood alone still spinning the balls, marvelling at the simplicity.

There was a thud which woke me. It was barely light, and I was on top of the covers. The book had fallen on the floor. Shivering I climbed underneath the duvet and snuggled back into a brief, light sleep.

CHAPTER 30

Here but not here

I was at work before the first cake had entered Ruth's mouth. She was so surprised there was a delay in the journey. From hand. To mouth.

I did wonder why she ate so much. Or why so many cakes. Maybe it was the sugar, or perhaps she didn't eat at home, or she didn't like what there was at home? Who knew? But cakes weren't the best to eat in large amounts - which Ruth did, effortlessly.

'What happened?' Ruth was wide eyed.

'What d'you mean?'

'You're never here this early,' she offered with a half-smile, looking partially awkward.

'I was just.... awake early.... I've not been sleeping well... and well.... I wanted to get in to sort the counter out, so I didn't have to rush.'

Ruth smiled her toothy smile and winked. It was then that the cake went in.

I think it did something to her as she sang a lot after eating cakes.

I set about putting the cakes out into the glass counter and the bread on the racks behind. Everything was just so. I viewed from the other side of the counter. It always looked different. Less messy from that side. I wondered if it was the glass. Or because there were labels on the backs of the trays. Or was it just a different angle being a customer?

'What are you doing Ags?'

'I just thought the cakes look better this side.'

Ruth's eyes widened. She moved quickly round.

'Wow. I think you're right. Even the bread pudding looks yummy.'

She headed back round and towards the tray.

'Ruth! No... you can't... I mean it will ruin the display.'

She reddened. And went head down to the kitchen.

'Sorry,' I echoed after her. What was I doing? I sounded like Tracey. But she will just get bigger and bigger and so many cakes can't be good for her. But then... who was I to speak? All of that Russian Pride I consumed.

I held my face for a moment. We were supposed to be going to the market after work.

I moved round behind the counter and headed towards the kitchen. The bell jingled above the door.

I could see Ruth in the kitchen looking sad and hovered before I slowly turned.

'Are you okay dear?'

'Hi Betty. I'm good. You ok? You're alone today?'

'Yes, just me. My dear Albie is in hospital.'

'Oh no... I hope it's nothing too serious?'

'Well, I think we have done well to get this far... it's time to move on to the next bit. Now can I have my tea and cake please dear, at the table.'

'Of course, yes.'

I watched her hunched walk. Small steps. Over to the table she sat at with Albert every day. I felt sad for her that she was alone. A daily occurrence that was so different today. I made her tea and put the cake on a plate with a napkin with huge daisies on it.

'Are you sure you're okay Betty?' I put the plate down and the tea.

'Yes dear. Why wouldn't I be?'

'Well... I just thought.... Albert in hospital...you might be a bit......sad?'

'Oh no. I'm okay. Albie and I have a special connection.'

I looked at her waiting.

'It means, dear, that we know we won't be apart even if we are apart.'

'I'm not sure what you mean?' I sat down opposite.

Betty looked at me like I had arrived from Mars.

'You can't sit there dear because Albie is sitting there.'

'Oh sorry,' I stood. 'Sorry, I..'

'You can sit there,' she gestured to the seat diagonally across from her.

There was silence as she sipped her tea and took the tiniest bite from her angel cake.

'But Albert is still with us?'

'Yes of course dear. He's in St Mary's Hospital. I left him and came here as I promised I would.'

'Oh, you've been to see him already. It's so early.' I was confused.

'Let's talk about something else. Albie will get frustrated if we talk about him like he's not here.'

I wasn't sure what to say. Silence was filled by Betty's small nibbles.

Saved by the door opening. I excused myself and went to serve.

More customers came for which I was grateful. Betty waved as she left without paying but I didn't have the heart to ask her for it. Who knew what was happening with Albert, but as long as Betty was happy.

I was conscious that the day was moving on and I was supposed to be going to the market with Ruth but we hadn't spoken and each time I had caught her eye from the front to the kitchen she looked sad.

As the queue tailed off, I took the opportunity to go to the toilet.

'Ruth ...are you okay?'

She didn't look up.

'I'm okay.'

'You've been really quiet today. I'm sorry if I offended you this morning.'

'It's okay. I know I'm fat and shouldn't be eating cakes.'

It was the truth, but I wasn't going to agree to it. I didn't feel I could. I think cakes are her whole life. They make her happy. Who am I to decide what is right or wrong for her.

'Shall we go to the market and buy something nice? You like the jewellery, don't you?' She nodded. 'Let's go and see what's there.'

Half smiling, she looked up and with a glint in her eye, 'okay'.

It was to be the most life changing afternoon, but it took me a while to realise.

CHAPTER 31

The Dress

By the time we left the bakery we were in tears with laughter. Mostly because Ruth had a cake in her mouth when Tracey stopped by as she was passing. Well, she said it was because she was just passing but I think perhaps she was checking up.

Tracey was not so kind about Ruth's passion, but it somehow didn't impact Ruth when Tracey was sharp with words. Ruth would smile and walk away. Impervious to the sharpness.

We cleared the counters and cleaned quickly. Looked back, looked at each other and nodded. It was good.

As we stepped outside the warmth of the sun caught my face and I turned to face it.

'We're going this way…' it was a question and an order all wrapped up in her way.

'To the market we go.' I checked my bag to make sure I had the book to return to the stall owner. I would find out his name today and pay for a book this time.

'What you going to get Ags?'

‘I’m not sure. What about you?

‘I really want some of the jewellery. You know the pretty pink ones. I like those. I haven’t got any and would really like some.’

‘You would look pretty in the pink. Not that you’re not pretty without them but they will add to it.’

She stopped and looked at me.

‘I know I’m fat Ags. But that don’t make me ugly. You drink a lot and I eat cakes.’

It hit me quite like a random smack in the face. *You drink a lot.* It echoed. *You drink a lot… you drink a lot….you drink a lot.* I had never heard this from a friend. Mum had always made comments but that was Mum. But Ruth. I didn’t know how to respond, and my thoughts frenzied around looking for an excuse to give for my drinking. There was none. I truly wanted to say, ‘I don’t really, just now and again,’ but I knew that it wasn’t quite true. I had drunk most nights and it wasn’t just one drink. Until recently that was.

I could feel her looking at me.

'It's a lovely day isn't it?' I almost laughed at her trying to divert the moment.

'It is,' I smiled. Still pondering the drink. The drink. The drink.

We wandered into the market. 'Ags look.' Ruth pointed to the second stall which was glittering with pink jewellery. A few stalls further was the book stall. It was an instant magnetic effect. It sparkled to me as much as the jewellery stall.

I noticed my hands starting to tingle. A funny sensation again, like somebody running a feather up and down my fingers and palm. It was both peculiar and familiar. I felt the urge to tell Ruth but then I worried she would think I had gone completely bonkers. Maybe I had; I wasn't even sure what it was. Perhaps it was a medical condition. I would look at that later.

We meandered to the bright powerful pinks and spent a long period of time trying different necklaces and bracelets on Ruth. First a thick one which seemed to exaggerate her own thickness, so I steered her towards the gentler ones which matched her beaming gentleness.

As we were trying on and laughing, I felt something. That feeling you get when somebody is watching you. Or maybe I saw him out of the corner of my eye I wasn't sure. He stood, tall and thin, at the front of the book stall. Looking along the lines of the stalls but seemingly straight at me. I felt awkward and turned my back, but the feeling continued until I turned around completely and waved in the general direction. As I did, he greeted somebody with a smile. I felt redness rise through my neck and into my face.

'Ags are you okay, you look very hot? What do you think of this one then? They don't really match but I like the chunky bracelets and this pretty one with the heart.'

'I.... um....I like them. I love them. They look great.' I was distracted again. Feeling ridiculous. It was becoming a theme today. Why would anybody be looking at me anyway?

By the time I had come back to the stall and Ruth mentally, she had bought both items and was wearing them proudly.

'D'you fancy something to eat?' I could see her eyes hinting towards the donut stall.

'I don't but you go ahead. I just need to return this to the book stall as we go past it.' I hoped that the man hadn't seen me waving like an idiot. Perhaps I could just slip the book back with a quick thank you. Or maybe I should just keep it.

We made our way to the donuts. Ruth speeding up as we got closer.

'Agnes?' The voice was deep and warm. Not one that I recognised.

Ruth and I both turned.

The tall man was right behind us. His smile exposing slightly wonky teeth. One of those smiles that can only be explained as horsey. His eyes tore straight into mine, and I, equally, was mesmerised by their light blue, watery effect. He bowed slightly but still kept the eye contact.

'It's good to see you again.'

I could feel Ruth looking at me. Probably willing me to say something but nothing came.

'Did you... read the book?'

'Err..... the book?..... yes, yes I did... I read it.'

'Good.' He nodded with some sort of approval.

An elbow gently nudged me. I looked at Ruth who was grinning wildly at me as though she had just seen her favourite cake.

'It was good. Very good. I.... er....I read it in one sitting. Such a powerful book. Oh.... In fact, I thought I should bring it back as I didn't pay for it.'

I pulled the book out along with some tissues and bits of paper that Ruth scrambled to pick up.

'Oh no, no you must keep it. It is a rare one that I enjoy sharing with others. Especially when they are on their way.'

Still, I stood transfixed with little to say. I was caught in a moment of not quite knowing I was here, or where I was.

'Would you like to look at my other rare books? There are some quite amazing ones.'

I nodded stupefied.

Ruth queued for her donuts and wandered off to a nearby stall that sold clothing. I followed the thin man to his stall where we sat. He opened up a treasure trove, dressed up as a box which was full to the brim with old books.

He looked at me intensely. The eyes boring into me and horsey smile almost jokingly laughing. 'Pick one.' He sat back and held his chin in between his first finger and thumb. Watching me.

Whilst the books were largely greys, brown and blacks, their sizes differed and the page edges were gilded with many different colours. I had never seen books this old before and was half afraid to touch them.

I lifted one out and picked the book beneath which was gilded with a violet colour. It looked pretty 'Always with you' sprung out from the cover in sparkly letters. The author's name was missing but the initials G.A. were underneath.

I held it out.

'Beautiful. That was one of my first reads of these particular books. You keep it. Read it.'

'But these must be worth something – I need to pay you for it.' I worried.

'No, no. It's a gift. Or bring it back when you've read it.'

We were interrupted by a customer.

I opened the book and flicked through to the opening chapter.

From the beginnings of energy to the circus of your guides. The joy and love of your angels. From your very own guide.

I sat and watched him serve the customer. This man, who I had suddenly realised knew my name, but I didn't have a clue of his. Comfortable, I sat as though I had always sat there, watching his graceful, slow movements and the ease with which he interacted with the customers, and seemed to know exactly which book they were after. The way that he looked very much straight into their eyes and most looked away, but I knew why.

'Agnes,' I was nudged and rudely brought back to the moment. 'Come and have a look at this dress. I think it would look lovely on you.'

I reluctantly let Ruth led me to the clothes stall. The dress was pretty. Knee length, pink, yellow and light green shapes all intermingling. 'Go on Ags, try it on,' she ushered me in to the makeshift changing room at the back of the stall.

I stood awkwardly; unaccustomed to wearing dresses, so pulling the hem down expecting it to go further. It was also a little bit low cut and I felt exposed.

‘Are you in it?’ Ruth whispered from the other side of the curtain.

‘Yes… well…almost’. She didn’t give me a moment to hide. The curtain whipped open.

‘Oh my God you look delicious.’ Somehow, I felt more like a cake. A fondant iced one.

It was her loud exclamation that drew the attention of the stall holder and passers-by who seemed to be excited to take a look at this delicious cake. The attention made me step back further.

‘Ruth! Shut the curtain.’ Before she registered my embarrassment and let go of the curtain, I looked out to see the tall man looking straight at me. He tilted his head and smiled.

The curtain came down and I could breathe. I looked in the mirror at the cake dress. At myself. It fitted my body like a glove.

I peered out from behind the curtain before I came out. Hoping that nobody was there but Ruth. I was relieved to see she was alone. Hanging the dress back on the rail I felt Ruth behind me.

'You really should get it, it looks lovely. Everyone said so.'

'Yes, but I don't think so.' I looked down… fiddling with the hem of the dress.

'Well, you might one day. I mean you might feel like it looks good if you put it on at home. I've done that with the necklaces.'

'Do you think so?'

She nodded her head like a child, a grin spread wide on her face.

I didn't have a dress. All I had was jeans and t shirts and …. nothing that was pretty, really.

Two minutes later I exited the stall with the dress. They were starting to pack away, and I was panicked for a moment that I hadn't said thank you to the tall man for the book that I clutched with its sparkly letters.

Standing at the book stall, or what had been the book stall, I felt a twinge of sadness. He had gone already. Why I felt sad I don't know. Just…. something.

We wandered up to the top of the road and went our separate ways. Ruth clutching her jewellery. And me with my sparkly book and cake dress. I smiled for the first time in a while.

CHAPTER 32

Finding Agnes

The weekend was written off by persistent rain. But it gave me time to read and to try on the dress and see how it really felt.

I spent much of the weekend in my dress, in my room. From dancing around to laying reading my new book from the market.

Opening the first pages I, once again, became aware of the tingling in my hands. It had intensified from last time. I placed the book down on the bed and looked at my palms then at the book which seemed to sparkle. The sensation almost stopped. That was odd. I picked up the book again and immediately the tingling returned. Maybe it was the cover on the book; made of some material that caused this?

I dismissed it and started to read. I read on.... and on....... until the light started to fade. The story taking me on a journey with a girl who seemed unable to fit in with those around her. Visiting incredible places. I felt myself there with her. Taking in the grandest and most astonishing beauty. And the best moment, to find that she had a friend – a guardian angel – who was with her all the time.

There was a flicker from outside as the streetlight came on. It was hard to put the book down. I was fascinated by the thought that we aren't actually alone. Ever. My eyes started to feel heavy, but I forced them open so as to read on.

My side lamp was on. The room chilly. The duvet tucked tightly around me. A tapping drew my attention away from the book. Regular. On time. Tap, tap, tap.

The light from outside drew shadows of the tree on the wall. Clearly defined with strong branches reaching out at all angles. I followed the line of the trunk and noticed a bump towards the base. As I watched, it started to move. First a leg. Swinging out and back. Followed by an arm. Both the leg and arm. I rose up on to my elbows to look closer. It looked like somebody was there. And yet it was just a shadow.

I sat up and looked down to find that I was still wearing the dress. I stood up and fiddled for the zip.

'No, don't do that,' the voice echoed around the room.

I froze and moved my eyes slowly from one corner of the room to the next. Bringing my hands down, I sat on the bed. Waiting.

A tiny movement again from behind the tree. A tall man dressed in a ringmaster outfit stepped into the room. I gasped for some air. What was this? Who was this?

He bowed. 'Hello Agnes.' The gentle voice was at odds with the appearance. 'I know it's hard to speak at moments like this, but it was time for me to come and say hello.'

His eyes were brown and his smile big. Like a horse. It reminded me of the tall man....I must find out his name.

'Oh.... There's no need to be afraid. I'm here as I always am. But you just don't normally see me. I do rather love your wonderful dress. You look absolutely sparkly. Don't you think?'

I found no voice.

'Sorry, yes, I forgot. I think there might have been a moment of visual impairment, so I've tried to correct that. I mean that you should have a look at your beautiful self in the mirror. Come along.'

He nodded his head excitedly and gestured for me to step forward into the view of the mirror.

'It's ok, look.' He stepped to face the mirror and waved at his reflection, greeted himself and said how very wonderful he was looking.

I laughed a very quiet laugh. Unsure, but feeling it was necessary, I climbed off of the bed and made my way to the mirror.

'I'm Bob, and I am at your service.'

Bob! I tried to say out loud. The Bob? I gestured and tried to speak but nothing would come out.

'It's okay. It's okay. It's me.' His face was so happy it almost struck me as ridiculous. Why would this be okay? How could it possibly be that? It was late. I had a strange man, dressed as a ringmaster, in my bedroom, who wanted me to look at myself in a dress in the mirror?

I stood with my head in my hands. Wishing it to stop.

'Agnes. The market today. When you tried this wonderful dress on. Did you see what happened?'

He knew about the market. How was that possible? I unburied my head.

'It's ok. I love you, Agnes. I can see you have a little bit of way to go but we can do this together. The book holds the answers. It's a tremendous read all about us.' He beamed proudly.

How on earth could this man be with me all the time and seemingly know so much about my day. And then it came to me. The book. The guardian angels. I scrabbled around for a pen and paper.

Scrawling quickly.... *Are you my guardian angel*?

He nodded furiously and with the biggest smile.

'Really?'

He nodded again.

'But how is that possible?'

'Oh, darling Agnes. You just have to trust. I am yours and there are lots of us looking after lots of you.'

'People?'

'Yes, everybody.'

I tried to think of anybody who I had spoken to who might know about this but, after a long think, nobody came to mind. I had either gone completely bonkers, or I was dreaming.

'And yes, you may think you've gone barmy, but I can tell you that you have 100% not.'

I wondered if …. If it were true…. and only if…. what did that mean?

'Well, Agnes. Imagine you can have anything that you would like. Well to be exact, your thoughts are what we like to listen to. We can help you with anything. Absolutely anything. We can make trains late or we can make them early. Hmmm that's not a very good example.'

Now I was beginning to wonder if all this was indeed true, was Bob a good one? And how do you tell a good guardian angel from a bad one? Are there any bad ones?

'Oh, yes, well none of us are bad Agnes.' There was a touch of indignation in his response.

It was at this moment that it dawned on me that I was not speaking. Not at all. And yet Bob was answering my thoughts. He could hear everything that I was thinking. Everything!

Which means. Oh my gosh, what if I think bad things?

He grinned. 'Nothing is a bad thing, Agnes. That's the jolliness of it all. No right or wrong. You can have whatever you think about.'

I wasn't sure. If that was the case, then I would need to be careful what I thought about. But I'm not sure that was possible. I didn't have that much control over my thoughts and sometimes...

'No, no, no Agnes. Don't you worry. I am here to make sure you find your way to your very best gifts. And to your most wonderful friends. But most of all I am here to help you find your way to you.'

I stopped and looked at Bob. *To find my way to me?*

'Yes, my lovely Agnes. This is the best bit. Finding Agnes.'

CHAPTER 33

Touched

A loud beeping shifted me out from a warm dream. I reached for the alarm only to find the stop button was already off. The sound was coming from outside. A car alarm. I was laid on my bed in the cake dress. No covers. The hairs on my arms standing up as the cool air drifted in through the slightly open window.

I looked around the dimly lit room unsure if I would see anyone still present and hoping not to as that would mean it wasn't a dream. And if it wasn't a dream...well...there was a strange person in my room. Called Bob.

I sat upright. The clock loud and proud at 3.33am. The light from these numbers and from the streetlight wasn't enough to show me the whole room. I feared the corners. Lunging for the bedside lamp I knocked it over. Another thud echoed to the side of my bed. I was swiftly under the covers and pulling them in tightly. What if somebody was in here? What if I had gone mad? What if somebody came and caught me, in bed, in a dress? Well, that wouldn't be unusual in terms of going to bed fully dressed if I had had a drink of course. But.... What if?

'Agnes?' I spoke out loud. Just checking I could speak. And again louder. 'AGNES?'

Nobody responded. But it was my name so of course they wouldn't.

'Bob?' I tried. I had never fully appreciated the loudness of silence until that moment. And that it had a piercing quality to it. Unsure what I would do if I got a response but finding some calm in talking out loud, I continued.

'Are you there? Because if you are I would like to know. I mean it would be good to know if I wasn't alone in the room.'

Would it? Would it be good to know you idiot? Not really. I don't even know who Bob is.

'Agnes, just get up and turn the light on and take the dress off and get into your pjs and go to sleep.... You're being stupid,' I muttered harshly to myself, with eyes still scouring the room.

Throwing the duvet cover off I swung my legs out. My heart raced. I picked up the lamp, set it on the bedside table and turned it on. As I did this a gust of wind blew the curtains gently into the room, making them float out and return like a Mexican wave. I watched and waited, mouth open, breath held.

Nothing else happened. The silence became less deafening. And I laid with my light on until I went back to sleep. A sleep that felt light as I waved in and out, tensing and relaxing.

I woke at eleven o'clock. As I blearily looked around, I saw the cake dress hanging happily from my wardrobe door.

CHAPTER 34

Walking in the light

All I could think about was how I wanted to get back to the market and see the man from the book stall. The only day I could go was Friday. There was no way I was getting out of Tracey's eyesight earlier in the week.

Ruth wore her jewellery to work with pride and took it off as soon as Tracey was around. I wore my dress into work on the Monday but didn't take it off.

'I don't think that's suitable for work,' was the crispy comment.

I didn't have anything else to wear so it stayed.

All day was a continuous repeat of, 'What a beautiful dress, you look lovely.'

Tracey's face was sour. Nothing I did was right. On Tuesday I squidged two separate bread puddings in the middle. Second time she went red in the face, and I could see Ruth in the kitchen holding her mouth to stop a cake exploding. I wasn't sure whether to laugh or cry.

And on Wednesday I mixed the cake positioning so the brownies were beside the Belgian buns. People did look confused when they came in but Tracey's cutting comments of derision in my direction left me wilting a bit.

On Thursday I was brightened by Betty coming in. Not with Albert. But *with* Albert I suppose? I took two cups of tea and two Belgian buns to her table.

'Thank you dear. You look lovely today,' Betty smiled up at me.

She gestured for me to sit in the seat diagonally from her and placed the second bun and tea opposite her.

She exhaled and looked straight ahead.

'Albie said he liked your dress. The one you wore the other day.'

'Okay. Thank you. Tell him I said thank you.' I had no idea how to handle this situation. How Albie could even possibly know I had worn a dress since he hadn't been in the bakery…I did not know.

'Tell him yourself,' she offered.

Flustered, I stood quickly, 'Sorry Betty .... I have to serve it's really busy.' I left her sat at the table looking after me, then muttering something to absent Albie.

'You can't just sit with customers making small talk. Can you cut some bread? Thin slice for Mr Prince and then do a medium cut for Mrs Takershall. Make sure they are bagged and sealed. Don't forget to make sure the crumbs are out from underneath the cutter, or they will get stuck to the loaf and we can't have that. Also, I need you to clear the tables. There's empty cups and plates everywhere.

I looked and saw one plate and cup lounging on a table. The rest were clear.

I happened to look over at Betty who looked above her glasses and winked at me having clearly heard Tracey. I smiled and went around the counter.

'Are you okay Betty. Shall I take your plate?'

'Yes, but leave Albie's as he's just on the loo and will eat his cake when he comes back.'

The tea for Albert was half drunk. Was he having bladder problems in hospital? I didn't want to ask, to ruin the moments that she was having with him.

Then… it struck me that I had been having conversations with Bob. Who wasn't present either. Maybe Betty and I weren't that different. Or that this was, in fact, quite normal. That you can be with somebody even when they aren't present physically. Was that mad? Perhaps not.

I cleared the other table and pondered on the idea.

An older lady I hadn't seen before entered. She headed for the counter but then seemed to veer towards Betty.

'Oh, Betty my dear. I am so sorry to hear about Albert. That must have been a terrible shock. I do hope you are coping okay and that you are managing with the arrangements. If you are ever needing to talk deary I am always at the end of the phone.'

I stopped. Albert was dead? But… no… he was in hospital. I turned to Betty who had eyes like wells. Tracey was stood with her hands on her hips, looking at the elderly lady and then at Betty.

'Can I help you?' her sharpness turned the lady to the counter.

'Oh yes, yes … I would like four of those lovely scones, and four of the meringues.'

'Anything else madam?'

'No no, that's it.'

She left without so much as looking back at Betty who sat teary-eyed.

'Betty, are you okay?' I stood near to her.

'Oh yes, I'm okay dear, it's been a terrible time and seeing Beryl ... well ...' she stood.

'Can I help you?'

'No dear, it's okay. I will be fine. There is always sunshine and what's meant for you comes your way.'

I stood and watched her shift out of the bakery. She hadn't paid but I could hardly call her back and I was surprised Tracey hadn't stood in the doorway and demanded.

I wondered if I saw a tear in Tracey's eye for a moment. But this was brought to a halt.

'Well, don't just stand there girl!'

I busied myself, where there was no busy to make, and then went into the kitchen.

Ruth looked at me. ‘What happened?’ she whispered. ‘You look odd.’

‘I think I might have seen Tracey getting emotional,’ I whispered in return.

Ruth grinned.

‘What happened?’

I told Ruth the story of Betty and Albert. By the time we got to the end of it she was almost crying.

‘But what if he’s still here in the loo?’ Her look was so sincere I couldn’t allow myself to laugh.

‘What do you mean? He’s not here he’s ... well... actually...,’ I made my way round to the customer toilets. It was engaged.

After a three hour wait Tracey’s husband arrived and opened the door using a crowbar. That, in itself, was something I could never imagine happening in Tracey’s household. Otherwise, the toilet was empty.

CHAPTER 35

Detachment

It was Friday and I woke excited. I put on the cake dress, sat in front of the mirror and put on some eyeshadow. A little lip gloss from old. I looked different. Somehow more… ladylike.

Descending the stairs was done with slow, gentle steps. I hoped that I wouldn't have to speak to Mum and have a third degree. I wasn't lucky.

'Where exactly are you going? You look like a trollop.'

I was taken aback. This was beyond Mum. A trollop?

'What's the matter Mum? That's not very nice.'

'Well look at you. I've never seen you like this. What has happened to you girl?'

'Nothing has happened Mum, I'm going out after work so just trying to look after myself.'

'Like that… pfffff.'

I didn't respond. I knew that if I listened any longer, I would start to believe it and I didn't want to do that today.

'Agnes!'

I put my shoes on and walked out of the door.

'AGNES!!'

I didn't look back. It was Friday and it was a good day. I was going to the market to get another book, and everything was going to be good. Nothing would stop this.

I walked briskly to work. Feeling people looking. In cars. Walking by. Looking out of windows in houses. What was this?

It took me 5 minutes less to get to work. Ruth stood with the door open wide eyed.

'Wow. You look amazin'!'

I fluttered my eyelids.

The day flowed through seamlessly. No Betty, but sometimes she didn't come in on a Friday anyway. I checked the book was in my bag. When I touched it I felt a surge of warmth. I felt excited to see the tall man and the book stall. Like I was expecting something.

'What are you doing Ags? You've been funny today. Are you still wanting to go to the market?'

‘Oh my God yes… I mean…. Yes … I’m looking forward to it. Maybe they will have some bracelets to match what you already have.’

She shrugged her shoulders and grinned. Did a little excited jig and returned to the kitchen.

Staring out of the window I watched the cars go by. Windows down, arms sticking out, allowing the sun to catch their exposed skin. Tapping to the beat of the car radio.

I was halted by a grinning Hagrid at the window. Smiling I put my nose up to the window which made him step back and screw up his face.

One Belgian bun and he was off down the road.

CHAPTER 36

Releasing

The market felt different today. The stalls seemed less inviting. Less sparkly I suppose. I could see Ruth looking avidly for the jewellery but all the stalls at the beginning were material or hardware.

'Ags, I think we might have the wrong day.' We both laughed.

I was anxious to get to the book stall but didn't want to rush. As we got further along, I could see the donut stall up ahead. I nudged Ruth and pointed. Her face lit up though she still searched for the bling of sparkly jewellery as we went.

Drawing closer I saw that the stall next to the donuts was fruit and vegetables. I stopped.

'What's the matter Ags?'

'I.... I .... thought the book stall was next to the donuts.'

'It is. Well, it was last week. Maybe it's moved Ags. Come on.'

Ruth ordered her donuts while I spoke to the fruit and veg owner.

'No love, it's fruit n veg this week. I think he was only here for a few weeks. I mean nobody's really interested in books as much these days maybe.' He laughed. I stood straight-faced.

'It was just a temporary stall. He's got a shop up in London I think,' the donut stall girl offered.

I remember a similar feeling with Billy. A panicky feeling. And a sense of blood draining from me, emptying. I wasn't sure why. Everything went a little blurry and I felt lost.

'But I had the book......' I held it in my hand and looked up to find Ruth stood in front of me. I fought back tears.

'Oh Ags, there might be another one. Here, have a donut, it'll make you feel much better.'

I took the donut and put it whole in my mouth.

I don't really remember much about the rest of the market as I was consumed by the thought that I should have said something to the tall man. Found out his name. But I hadn't. And that was my own fault. I should be more forceful. More confident. Though I'm not. That's why nobody stays. That's why I looked stupid stood in the cake dress in the middle of the market trying to understand why on earth I had even worn the dress. How stupid I must look.

Ruth was talking but I couldn't even bring myself to listen. It was just muffled sounds in the background.

She hugged me goodbye at the top of Moon Street. I stood for a while and then decided tonight was a Russian Pride night. I scuttled off past the bakery and headed towards home and the corner shop. Picked up my favourite and was out on the corner and looking across at the park. It was a warm evening, and the park was quiet.

I walked quickly hoping to find a shaded spot or maybe even Bob's bench free. All I wanted was to feel the warmth of the alcohol trickling down my throat and into my stomach. I sat under a tree facing towards the sun.

The familiar feel of the bottle was quite comforting. I kept it in the bag and twisted the lid off slowly.

The taste on my lips and tongue was intense as I closed my eyes. I allowed a small amount to find its way down the internal path. While the sun warmed my face.

'I don't think you really want to be doing that do you?' A warm inquisitive voice followed by a familiar aroma drew me gently back to the space where I was sat.

I choked as I turned to see Hagrid's face right beside mine.

'Hagrid.' Tears gently trickled down my cheeks.

'Come on, come on…,' putting his arms around me and pulling me in to his knotty beard I let myself cry.

The silence was comforting. The largeness too. We sat beneath the tree like this for a while before Hagrid spoke.

'Sometimes, things go up and down a bit. A bit like a ride on the sea. And we have to ride the waves.' He motioned the waves with his hands.

'But I can't seem to keep people near me. I've been having these strange dreams. It's all like I'm doing everything wrong. I thought Billy liked me and then he went away. I thought I had found somebody who understood me at the market, and he's gone away too. And I'm just here.'

Holding me back a little and looking right into my eyes, like he was exploring a very interesting bin, 'I'm here too Agnes.'

'Yes but…. why do people keep coming and then going quickly? Is there something wrong with me? I'm just too sensitive to everything Hagrid. I couldn't live with Dan because he was switched off. He never heard me. And then when I meet people who I think are more sensitive they don't stay.' I felt my lip quivering. 'And now this just sounds like I feel sorry for myself... it's not ...I don't...I just..'

'Ssshhhssshhhh.'

Again, I was amongst the curliness. Being held. Being loved.

'I've got a story. You want to hear it? Yes, course you do.' He continued to stroke my hair.

'I... even when I was a small boy .... Used to feel like it would be really nice to find somebody to have as a friend all the time. Somebody to be with, like a twin brother or something like that. It was just me, me mum and me dad; they didn't like each other and then they went and died. So, I lived with my Aunty Joan. Just me and her. She never had kids and it was hard cause she tried too hard to get me right. So, when I was 16 I left. I just went.'

Hagrid paused and looked off into the distance. I looked up at him. 'Where did you go?'

No response.

I ruffled his arm. 'Hagrid?'

'It's Sherbet.'

‘Sorry… Sher..bet.’ I let out a small sniffy laugh.

‘So where was I? Yeah. I ended up at a Salvation Army place. Hostel type thing. Well, there was some good and bad uns in there. But I met a girl.’

I sat up. Hagrid… with a girl…

‘Well, she was larger than life and I worshipped the ground she walked on. And if she had been the same about me it would’ve been a very fine romance. Not so. But I admired her. She never looked to anybody for anything, and she was always happy as Larry. She was like glowing all the time. You know.’

I didn’t, but I still nodded.

‘Thing is Agnes. She was my biggest lesson. She taught me that you have to love yourself first. ‘Cause if you don’t, ain’t nobody else going to do it for you. When you love yourself and you feel safe with yourself….. see…I didn’t….I was looking for somebody to keep me safe or me heart safe. And this doesn’t happen. I spent a week or two looking for a replacement after she’d gone off to do her thing and then blow me if I had the same experience again. And again. Took me a while to get it but eventually…. It sunk in like.’

‘I’m Schubert and I’m good as I am.’ He held his arm across his head as if receiving an award.

I giggled. But this was halted by the questioning look.

‘It’s not an easy thing to do Agnes but I think you’re getting there. And when you’re ready, you won’t need to turn to this.’ He picked up the bottle. ‘Only when you’re ready.’

I looked down at my hands and fiddled with my fingers. The thought that I had sat in the park and started drinking directly from the bottle washed deep shame over me.

‘Don’t go beating yourself up about it now, ‘cause that will make you feel like you’ve done something wrong when you haven’t. It will happen... you mark my words.’

The silence was holding.

‘Why does it hurt so much Ha... Sher....can I call you Sherbie?’

‘Yes, you may.’ He smiled for what was the first time I had seen. ‘It’s ‘cause you haven’t quite got connected with this.’ He pointed towards the middle of my chest. I looked down unsure.

‘When you sit in your heart Agnes.... That’s where all the magic is. Don’t listen to what’s going on up here.’ He tapped his bird's nest of wild hair. 'Always go with what your heart wants.... Always.'

'How do I know what my heart wants? How is that possible?' I panicked. I didn't have a clue. It seemed good advice.

'Let go of everything Agnes. Don't be attached. It will always be the first thing that you think, feel, sense. Always go with that. And you gotta trust yourself.'

I wept again. But this time with a sense of release. That I had somehow found a new way to go.

Though the idea of alcohol, or even just not being here anymore was comfortable, I knew it wasn't the way I wanted to go. It didn't feel like the right way now, at least.

'Sherbie?'

He looked at me stroking his beard.

I fumbled looking up at him and looking down into the depths of my well stocked handbag. I pulled out the book and riffled through the first pages. Fanned the whole book, then held it upside down shaking it out. The small card fluttered out, landing on the grass.

'Circinus Books.' I read aloud. '32 Cecil Street, London.'

I looked at Hagrid.

'I think I'm going to go and find it. I've just a feeling that I should.'

He winked at me. Stood up and held out his hand to help me up.

'I gotta go get some dinner at the church. Come on, you need to go home and get imagining yerself up in London.'

We said our goodbyes. Again, I got that hollow feeling but this time I let it through. I love you, Agnes. I love you; I love you, I love you. Thank you Sherbie, Hagrid. I held my hands together in prayer.

CHAPTER 37

Journey

I watched fields go by. Then houses that passed quicker than I could blink. A fuzzy view that made my eyes repeatedly come to centre.

There were a handful of people in my carriage, but there may as well have been none. The silence was comfortable. I felt an inner tremble at the thought of arriving in a strange place. Both excitement and anxiety. What if I got lost? What if somebody ran off with me? *Don't be ridiculous Agnes... but still...What if I couldn't find it?*

Just ask someone. Ruth had said this to me on repeat all week. But each time was like the first. *It's okay to ask for help Agnes.*

The train rode quietly. Effortlessly. And in a blur, I was pulling into Charing Cross Station.

Alone in the carriage I sat rigid. Why had I come here? Was it the best idea? Of course, of course it was. I needed to see the book shop and the tall man. This edged me over fifty percent in favour.

The warm air was bottled in the tunnelled area of the platform. I looked back and could see the track extending back to where I had come from and forward to the barriers, which would allow me to begin my adventure.

I stood and looked past the barriers at the people milling, waiting, looking up for some information. More incoming railroaders paraded in my mind. *Should I go through the barrier? What if I get lost or can't find the shop? How am I going to get to the shop?*

Then a reminder floated in. *Ask, Agnes, it's okay to ask for help.*

I walked up to the barrier. Put my ticket in the slot. A bleeping noise and 'seek assistance' showed up. I looked around. Suddenly regretting. *See.. told you.. it was a mistake... even the barrier is keeping you out.*

'This way.' A man wearing a blue uniform with Network Rail emblem beckoned me.

'It said seek assistance. I'm not sure why I ....'

He held out his hand. I passed the ticket over. It wasn't quite the welcome I was expecting.

The barriers opened. I walked through and took the ticket back.

'Move along please.'

This wasn't the person I needed to ask for help. Maybe there would be a policeman, they're usually helpful. I followed the exit sign through an archway, which led me to a cobbled area. Taxis. Black ones like in the films. A man sat on a sleeping bag with a sign 'please, I'm homeless, any loose change appresheated.' I looked away trying not to give it my attention. I didn't have enough money for myself let alone giving it away.

I decided that the best way to do this was to ask a taxi driver and if I had enough money that's what I would do.

'Excuse me.' I banged on a taxi driver's window.

'I'm booked,.' he shouted and gestured to the one behind.

I hurried along. The driver's window was halfway open. 'Excuse me, I wonder if you can help me.'

'Well, that depends luv,' he laughed.

‘I, um...’ I fumbled in my bag for the card. ‘I need to get to this address.’ He took the card looked and handed it straight back. ‘Jump in.’

‘Um...I need to know how much it is as I only have a little money.’

‘How much you got? Gonna cost you a ton.’

‘I’ve got £10.’ He laughed again and told me to get in.

‘This your first time in London luv?’

‘Yes, I’ve... come to see a friend.’ I thought he might laugh if I told him I had come to find a book shop. It’s hardly like the rest of the country doesn’t have them. Though this was an unusual one, I thought.

He hummed and whistled. I saw a multitude of signs and Nelson’s column, the National Gallery, theatres, both sides of the road. So many people wandering, stopping. And so many cars. It wasn’t long before he pulled over.

‘Cross the road here and just up there is an alley. That leads into Cecil Street.’

‘Oh, that was quick. How much is it?’

‘It’s on the meter luv. Tenner.’ I gave him my note and stepped out.

It felt vibrant, busy, alive and scary all at once. I had never been in such a busy place nor seen so many cars before. Beeping. People calling out, rushing around and others just strolling, engaged in chatter with their friends.

It struck me then that I was alone. I crossed the road and headed up towards the alley. Its narrowness made it darker, but it was a row of quaintness. Little shops with signboards outside. It felt like I had been transported back in time as I stepped tentatively into the alley and took a slow walk. The smell of bread and cakes came to me as I was halfway along. There was the tiniest cake shop. The Little Whisk. It made me smile and I looked in at the most amazing array of cakes. Much more spectacular than those we had in our bakery. There were swirls and colours beyond the realms of possibility of a cake shop in Purbrey. Ruth would want to eat the whole lot. I couldn’t wait to tell her and wished I could take her one home as a gift. Maybe next time. I surprised myself. As I got to the end of the alley there was another small road and opposite, I saw the sign ‘Circinus Books.’ The words written in swirls and curls and the hint of a sparkle.

In the window was a setup of the inside of a circus tent. Jugglers, clowns, tightrope walkers, lion tamers, unicyclist and a ringmaster right at the centre. As I stood looking, I noticed some of them moving. Just small moves. The ringmaster stepped forward and bowed as though acknowledging my presence. A cyclist rode back and forth and a clown had the biggest grin when he tripped over his enormous shoes.

Above the display I could see somebody moving. Looking in at the display.

I took a deep breath and opened the door into the shop. The light peered through the gap as I opened the door and then took me in whole as I stepped in.

My mouth open, eyes squinted and partially open at first, I was enveloped in rays of bright golden light. Pouring down, across and over, they hit the floor, walls, shelves. Expanding tubes of light flowing every possible way so that no corner was left untouched. Everything illuminated. No darkness. No shade.

I stepped in further. The brightness becoming less fierce so I could open my eyes a little more. I could see particles floating in each ray, floating gracefully in some spaces and frantic in others, as air shifted in and around. Colours existed on the edges of the rays, forming rainbow edges and expanding out further, opening up the room so it felt like it pulsated. Filled to the point of bursting with light. I felt myself filling up too. A warm feeling; joyful and safe.

As my eyes adjusted fully, I could see the books sparkling on the shelves. Vivid and alive. Almost moving. I walked closer to the books to reach out and touch. *Were they real? Was this real?* As I got closer, I could make out titles 'The Never End of the World', 'Wise Heart', 'The Gentle Voice'. Their beauty shining through in colours and letters. I reached out to touch them.

'Agnes?'

The sound of his voice was familiarly gentle. I turned. At first, I wasn't sure it was the same person. He looked younger.

'Agnes, it's you. How wonderful to see you.' His tone was gentle, surreal even.

I found myself lacking words.

'I hope you had a safe trip. It can be a little tricky to find us but you're here, that's so marvellous.' He clapped his hands together.

'You must have a good look around. These books here are just the beginning. There are so many more upstairs with such a different story.'

I looked up. A set of narrow wooden stairs twirled up to a balcony which stretched back a long way with more shelves of brightly coloured books. I stood as though magnetically pinned to the spot.

'Would you like a drink, Agnes? You've come a long way.'

'I.... yes please.'

'Robert!' a small voice called from the balcony.

'Yes?'

'Where is the one about the magic carpet? Where the boy has three wishes. I want to try that one.'

'Third shelf, 5th bookcase. It's got a lovely rose spine.'

I heard a chuckle.

'Take a seat, I'll make some tea.'

Perched on a stool I looked around. The deep warm of the wood shone as though it had been polished for days. I ran my fingers along the edge and watched a flutter of sparkles lift up and then settle. When I did it again, they stuck to my fingers. I tried to brush them off. As I was doing this he returned.

'Ah, you've been caught red handed,' he smiled and placed the teacup down. 'I just sprinkled those this morning. They do take an age to get off. So... Agnes. What made you decide to come and find us?' he stared into her eyes.

I wasn't sure about the word 'us.' It made me feel uncomfortable in some way. Was there a significant somebody else about to step forward? But then why would that matter. Hagrid's words echoed in my head....'Everything you look for in somebody else is already stored right in here'.

'I just wanted to come to London. I have never been and since I found your card in the book ...I felt I should drop in.'

'Ah, the book. How was it?'

I stalled. I wasn't sure if it was the light or if his features were so soft that they resembled a woman. And yet, when he turned to look another way... yes... he was surely a man.

'Oh.' I came back to the moment. 'It was amazing. I loved it so much I've got it .... ' I fumbled around in my bag. The bottomless pit of tissues. 'It's in here... yes.' I held it out. It was sadly less colourful than the books in the shop, but it still gave my hands that fizzy feeling when I held it.

He looked at the book and at me. 'It's a special one. There are more here. You should look around.' His hands seemed to climb the shelves behind, bringing down a sparkly silver book.

Covering it he hesitated, 'I think, Agnes, that you are ready for this.'

The air seemed so tense. I felt I couldn't breathe. Then from nowhere, I burst into tears.

Tissues came sliding across the counter as if this was a common occurrence. Maybe it was. Maybe I wasn't the first to feel like this. Like I could burst. But in a good way. The whole journey up to London and finding the shop had taken its toll.

'Sometimes...,' the gentle voice wrapped around me like cotton wool. 'We find what we are looking for in the places we least expect. More so, we find them in ourselves, and we don't know what do with them. But when we find them, we never lose them again.'

I wasn't sure I understood but I nodded my head anyway. The words reverberating in my head, some louder than others. FIND what we are looking for in PLACES we least expect. We FIND them in OURSELVES.... we NEVER LOSE them AGAIN.

I cried again. This time followed by a feeling of elation. Like my heart would burst with love.

'See?' He looked at me questioning.

'I am Robert, by the way.' He held out his hand.

I held out my hand gently taking his. It's smoothness unlike anything I had felt before. Velvety. And a tingly sensation as our fingers connected.

'I'm Agnes.' I felt stupid the moment I uttered the words. He already knew. There was little time to feel embarrassed though.

'Robert!' the small voice came from above in an atrium like area.

'I'm coming.' He released my hand and went to the stairs, running up them with grace and ease.

I turned back to face the counter and the shelves behind. The book Robert had brought down was sat in front of me. It's title 'The Star' sparkled.

I pulled it towards me and felt the fizzle in my palms. I grabbed it hungrily. What was in this book? Something that I needed to read. I felt a surge of energy as I opened it. In some way I suppose I expected some sort of magic to happen. Nothing did at that moment. I turned through the first pages which were largely blank. And then the next page 'You are exactly where you are supposed to be. Right here. Right now.'

A shiver went through my body. What if? *Here you go again Agnes*. Yes, but what if.... what if that was right? I'm exactly where I should be. I'm in the right place. I have always been in the right place that means, doesn't it?

'I think so.' the voice was gentle behind me.

'Sorry?' I turned. Robert stood behind me looking, head tilted.

'I think you're in the right place.'

'But I didn't say anything'

Robert smiled. 'You were talking to yourself quietly'

'No...... I mean.... was I?'

He looked towards the book.

'I knew you would like it.'

My whole body was a fizz. Like I was about to explode.

'Robert? What is this feeling I have with my hands? It's spreading into my body like.... Well...I don't know, it's like I've drunk three cans of Red Bull in a row.'

Robert chuckled. A funny childlike noise.

'That, my dear, is energy.'

'Energy?'

'What is all around us. Inside of us. What we are made of.'

'Air? Dust?'

'My Darling... it is more than all of us can comprehend.... Until we are ready. It brings with it colour out of the black and white and joy out of the colour. But there is joy to be found in the black and white.... This is where the shadow sits.'

‘The shadow?’ my mouth just slightly open. Could something possibly be this way?

‘We are light and dark Agnes… all of us. The dark bits are the shadow. We all have a shadow. You only have to check the light and look back. There it is.’

‘But that’s just me in the light.’

‘Ha ha… yes indeed. What about the soul? That too has a shadow. The wonderful pieces of us that feel so dark and desperate.’

I looked at Robert. What could be so wonderful about dark and desperate places? Why would you even consider this as some sort of good place? I felt the sting of tears. And also, the well of anger. Seemingly out of nowhere.

‘That’s not right,’ I stood up ready to exit. ‘How could you even say such a thing? People who go to dark and desperate places are in a very bad way, they want out. They don’t want to sit around in the hell of pain because it’s WONDERFUL. It’s not a joy ride. It’s not anything. It’s hell on earth…. who are you even…?’ The tears started to flow.

I stood helplessly rooted to the spot.

Slowly and gently, Robert walked around the counter.

'No don't come near me. I think I've made a mistake in coming here. It's just a shop. You're just a...... a....,' I looked at him. Exactly what he was I couldn't put into words. It was neither good nor bad. Nor nothing.

I had hoped. No, I had *wanted* to find something here. I wasn't sure what, but I hadn't wanted to revisit this feeling. This pain. This non understanding of where I had been.

Robert held out his hand. As he did so I noticed a tattoo on his wrist. A flower. The short stem and leaves on his hand leading up to his arm. It was a daisy. Long white oval petals and a warm gold swirling centre, being offered to me. There was something familiar about this. I held out my own hand but not to touch his. I didn't need to touch. As my hand neared his I could feel the tingling sensation, the fizz of 'energy' warming my palms, my hands.

So gently and warmly came the words, 'Everything is a gift, Agnes. Some in more sparkly wrapping. Some in dull, brown, well-worn wrapping. We cannot be one without the other. We cannot have the light without the dark. Or we simply would not recognise it as such. The sun rises bringing us the beauty of the day, the moon comes to show us the wonder of the night. The kindness of one person fills us with warmth. The ignorance and rudeness of another leaves us cool. Our joys and laughter lift us higher, and yes, we want to keep these... all of the time. But the hollowness of pain and sadness are what allow us to see the beauty of the joy. It is a gift.'

I needed to sit but I wanted to stand. I understood it but didn't want to. I wanted somebody to know how bad the pain was.

'But it was horrible. I mean it is horrible. I don't want to feel it.' I stood limp. Not even sure what I was saying or if it made any sense. Nothing was making any sense. Why couldn't we just be happy all the time? Why did people have to be rude or bad?

I moved back to the seat. Feeling raw. I wasn't ready to leave. I didn't want to.

Robert returned to the other side of the counter.

'ROBERT!' the demand from upstairs.

'I'll be right back.' He seemingly floated off again, up the stairs, to whoever had called.

I sat and stared at the counter. The book. In a daydream of thoughts. Good versus bad. Light versus dark. Yes. I suppose it wouldn't be the same if there was just a constant stream of light and no dark. The sameness of everything. Everyday repeating. No bad. Nothing to react against. And this seemed such an ideal way to be but what if it wasn't. What if I lived in that world? Where there was no comparison, just a steady stream of one thing? Would that not be dull? Would I really want that? Yes. And no. I let out a small laugh. What if we all said yes to everything?

Robert appeared without effort. 'Let me show you around the shop.'

I really wanted to talk some more but then felt ravaged by my own thoughts and welcomed the distraction.

Robert trailed his hand along the books as we headed to the back of the shop and to a corner which was well lit by a large ray of light. The books here seemed less interesting. The titles were a little grey.

'These are the very used ones. Some gems in there though.'

I sat in this corner and ran my hands over the books. Exploring the titles with my fingers. I pulled out a book titled

'Cartwheels for beginners.' I smiled at the memory of Billy. Flicked through it and put it back. As I did, I noticed the book next to it. It had a heart drawn on the back cover – an A and B split by the arrow going through the heart. I pulled the book out and traced the heart with my finger. 'The Circus Trick,' shone out as I turned it over. A gentle tingling sensation ran along my fingers, inviting me inside the front cover. Opening it up I could just about make out the scrawly writing of an inscription. 'To A, What is meant for us, will always find us again. Shine bright in the circus of this life. Until we meet again. My love always B x'.

I remembered the handstands with Billy. And wondered where he was now. Somewhere in London. What if I were to meet him?

'Did you find something good.' The voice was gentle but startled me.

'Oh, nothing...I mean.... This has a lovely inscription.' I held it out to Robert.

'Ah yes, 'The Circus Trick.' I have often wondered who the people were. Who loved deeply enough to set each other free,' he spoke with a tender hint.

'Do you think they didn't stay together?' I said hopefully.

Robert held the book between his hands and breathed in deeply. 'I think…. They were enough together that they could be apart and still feel the joy of having love.'

'But it would have been hard to let somebody go if they really loved them, wouldn't it?' I was becoming a bit stressed about the issue. They surely didn't love them if they let them go.

'It is this way sometimes. But if you truly love, without attachment, then this is true love. It may be a little uncomfortable, but it is the truth about letting them be the best of themselves. Letting them fly.'

'Oh… '. My thoughts drifted to Billy again and our brief encounter. Then to Robert when he disappeared from the market stall. And whilst it wasn't love…. Or was it? If this is what that love felt like I wasn't sure I wanted to do love. Maybe that was why Mum never had a partner after Dad had gone.

'ROBERT!' He smiled and shrugged his shoulders and moved to head back up the stairs.

'Who is that?' I asked before he had a chance to run up the stairs.

‘It’s my accomplice,’ he tilted his head thoughtfully.

‘Your accomplice?’ I repeated a little unnerved.

‘Where there is seriousness there has to be fun. That is the rule. There has to be opposite. Now we’ve looked at the serious side… let’s have a look at the fun side,’ he winked.

What could possibly be up the stairs was beyond me. And, as I walked away from the shop that day I wondered if I had been stupid or brave in following him up the stairs. The narrow, winding stairs that got narrower as we got to the top. Somehow it felt like home. Somehow, it felt safe.

Up there I found high bookshelves lining the room. A moving ladder was up against one shelf and at the very top was a very small elderly lady.

‘Robert!’ the elderly lady demanded.

‘I’m here’ he responded wearily but smiling up at her.

‘Oh!’ she looked and squinted through smudged glasses.

‘Hello,’ she shrilled at me.

‘Hi,’ I waved. I waved and I still wonder why. She was higher up I suppose.

'Mother, this is.... well...I will let her introduce herself.' He almost bowed to allow me to announce myself to this little woman stood up so high.

'I...am Agnes,' I announced rather proudly.

'Oh, jolly good. Well, I'm stuck, can you just get me down from here, otherwise I will call the police. I have been calling and calling and you just left me here.'

'Mother, we were having fun; remember gliding along the rails with the ladder.'

'That was your fun not mine,' she responded with a frown.

I found myself stifling a laugh.

He slowly climbed the ladder and helped her down graciously one step at a time.

At the bottom she looked up at him and smiled. 'Can we play it again dear? I do rather love it.'

'Of course, Mother.' He looked at her with what I could only describe as pure love. He just glowed with it.

I watched them slide along as he stood behind her making sure she was safe and held on.

I left them that way as it seemed like I had overstayed my welcome.

Leaving the shop, I felt the air close in around me. Air or energy? I wasn't sure. I walked back up the alley way. The shops were closed. The small cake shop window was clear and the blind down. I must bring Ruth here. I looked down and realised I was still holding the book. The Circus Trick.

CHAPTER 38

Reconnect

Where had I put my ticket? I unloaded bits on to the nearby window shelf, looking both ways to ensure nobody would come and steal anything. Not that a tissue ... and a used one at that...would be much worth stealing.

Nothing.

I felt my heart beat double time. What if I couldn't get home? I would be stuck in London. Forever. Turning back towards the bookshop my view was filled with a wrinkled t shirt, a grin and a wink.

'Hello lovely. Fancy seeing you here.'

Without hesitation I flung my arms around Billy's neck. Elated, scared, happy, sad. I was a ball of emotions. The flood of tears poured all over Billy's creased t-shirt.

'You're gonna drown us both in a minute. Let me take a look at you.' He held me at arm's length and looked me up and down. Nodding his head, 'Looking good Agnes... well... there's some dark stuff here...,' his gentleness was soothing as he wiped away my leaking make up.

'Still got the daisy you stole?' his cheeky laugh echoed along the lane.

I put my hands in my pockets expecting to feel the brooch. Instead, I felt a smooth flat oblong shape. I pulled it out. My return ticket.

Billy whipped it out of my fingers. 'What's this? Oh, so you think you're going back now? I've got news for you.' His hand slid into mine and he pulled me along the small lane out into the brighter light of the road.

With a wide and cheeky smile, he led me in and out of streets, along pathways, until we reached an opening in a square. There were people stood on boxes. Covered in colour and sparkles but no seams between clothes and skin. I found myself staring, waiting for the blink that never seemed to come as they held a pose in complete stillness.

Further along we came across a juggler. Billy joined in. Sometimes upright, sometimes upside down. Bringing in cheers from the circle around them. Their faces all with expressions of awe and excitement at what could possibly happen next. They became a double act for the rest of the performance while I merged with the framing audience.

The juggler collected the money thrown into his hat. Shook hands with Billy and moved on.

‘I should get the train now.’ I offered half-heartedly.

‘Nope, you’re not going anywhere yet.’ And then we were walking at a pace back towards the centre, across the main road and into a park.

We sat enjoying the coolness of ice creams, frothily circled, and not one, but two chocolate twirls sticking out like ears. It was the first time Billy had sat still. We watched as a band set up their instruments in the band stand, taking their time with music stands and making seats comfortable.

From the rumble and zoom of passing traffic to the smooth soothing sounds of tunes that sounded like they came from the 1940s, but were modern-day music.

I felt a gentle touch of another’s skin on my cheek.

‘You’re beautiful you know.’ Billy looked at me, inching round my face with his eyes.

I felt the heat rise. Unable to respond I looked down, but my chin was elevated back up again by his hand.

‘Don’t hide away Agnes.’ A mischievous grin spread over his face. ‘The perfect thief.’ He moved away quickly. ‘Come on let’s see your handstand.’

The sun started to shift down in the sky and after many tries, and one or two successes, the thought of home came to mind.

We lay watching the sun lower. Feeling the connection between us increase. An invisible cord of energy linking from one to the other.

‘Why don’t you come back with me? Just for a day?’ I asked.

Billy rested his head on his hand. Drawing pictures on my face with his eyes.

‘You scared to go back alone?’ he cocked his head and smiled.

‘What? No. No..I just thought you might like to see everyone again.’

‘I think we should cartwheel our way round the park.’ He was off before I could protest. A pause as he waited for me, but I chose to stay put and watched the spectacle of bedazzling showmanship that was Billy. His smile radiated out to all he passed.

Eventually, making his way back to me, breathing heavily, he bowed. I applauded, 'Bravo Bravo.'

The light sank gently as we walked to the station. The fizzing between our hands intensifying as we reached the entrance.

Our lips touched. Soft and warm. The ignition of fire in my stomach soared through me like a firework.

'See you again, lovely Agnes.' And he was gone.

I stood still holding the sensation. A lowering in my heart caught me. I held my breath as I realised that I didn't know when I might see Billy again. Or if I would see him again. But the feeling was not a bereft emptiness. More a gentle feeling of loss.

Stepping out of the entrance and back into the street I looked in the direction he had gone. The street lit now by twilight and streetlights, there was no mistaking the outline of his jaunty walk. It made me smile. My fingers traced my lip. Remembering. I would see him again.

I turned and took the feeling with me into the station, which had just two people standing looking at the departure board. Was it later than I thought? Nobody was going to Purbrey at least. Maybe I would have the train to myself.

‘The next train to Purbrey, calling at Gilfold only, will depart at 20…22 from platform two.’

All twos, how funny. Nobody else moved except me to platform two. The train seemed to be endless, but I followed my desire to be right at the front carriage. Next to the driver.

It seemed a long walk but as I got on the train the bleeping noise echoed through and the doors closed. I was accompanied again by silence. Lights on, which made it increasingly difficult to see what was outside.

We stopped at Gilfold. A couple got on. Their acknowledgement of my presence was followed by a shuffling up to the far end of the carriage. A steady increase in the volume of conversation drifted down towards me.

The air changing. Coldness or tension creeping in. I could see they were sat opposite each other but now looking outside. Shut off from one another. She was crying, silently. Not wanting to call attention but crying out for it. And he, oblivious, somewhere else entirely.

I felt I wanted to go and mend them. Reconnect what had been somehow lost. *‘Hi, I’m Agnes, it doesn’t have to be this way.'* Would probably be greeted with a sod off, mind your own business you weirdo. Who did I think I was anyway?

The silence remained all the way to Purbrey.

Just as we were approaching the station, the ding dong of a forthcoming announcement was followed by, 'Good evening ladies and gentleman. This is your driver speaking. Hope you've had a super journey on this very fast choo choo to Purbrey. All three of you. Don't forget your things. And don't leave your thoughts either. Have a safe onward journey. See you very very soon. Toodaloo.'

A blast of laughter escaped me. The humour didn't reach the couple.

I stepped out of one door and they the other. Two different exits.

CHAPTER 39

Return

Facing the house, I looked up at my room. The darkness, soon to be lit. The house seemed different to how I recalled. The windows upstairs looked down on me. Part open, as if creating eyelids. The lights were on downstairs. The letter box glinted in the streetlight, seemingly inviting me in.

The hall was cold, as always, and I could see Mum's legs extended out from the chair, crossed over at the ankles. She did this when she fell asleep in the chair.

Except today she hadn't quite got there and was watching the TV with a fixed gaze.

'Where you been?' her comment undirected as her gaze stayed at the TV.

'London.'

Her eyes on me now. 'London? What you doing going to London?'

'Went to see a friend. It was nice. It's really ... interesting?'

'Oh no, it's not safe up there. You need to be careful. Going swanning off to these places. What's wrong with Purbrey? Lots to do round here Agnes. No need to go to dangerous places like that.'

'Have you been there Mum?' My calm questioning and the use of 'Mum' paused her.

'No but it's not the place for a young girl.'

'Okay. I'm going to bed now. I'm tired. See you in the morning.'

I felt her eyes follow me. All the way until my feet disappeared at the top of the stairs. No further words.

My room was cool and clear as I entered. I pulled the window down leaving just a centimetre to allow in air... and a bat maybe.

Folding my clothes and leaving them neatly placed on the top of the drawers I stopped to look outside. Back at where I had been stood just now. I could see somebody or something. Hovering by the tree. The bushiness round the hair. Could it be Hagrid?

I lifted up the window and whispered loudly. 'Hagrid? Is that you?'

He shifted into the light of the streetlamp and smiled up at me. Whispering too, as much as he could. 'Just followed you 'ome to make sure you got here okay.'

I found myself giggling like a young girl and waving.

CHAPTER 40

Living in the light

Monday arrived. At the bakery before anyone else I stood and looked around the street. I was excited to see Ruth and tell her about my trip to London. Mostly about the small cake shop but also about Robert and what had happened. Well, some of it.

I saw her beaming at me from a distance. Then she wobbled and ran as fast as she could.

'Look at you! Tell me what happened Ags. You look strange. I mean good, strange.'

'It was amazing Ruth. I saw this lovely cake shop and I just know you would adore it. You must come with me next time.'

She looked at me and cocked her head to one side.

'I don't want to go to London. You could bring me one back though.' Her face joyful at the thought.

I told her about the book shop and the sparkly colourful books. Some details left for another time.

'What did your mum say?' she raised her eyebrows.

‘Oh…she didn’t say much.’

We were interrupted by Tracey coming in.

‘Oooo, what have you been up to Agnes. Bit glowy.’ She looked me up and down.

‘I went to London,’ I gushed, immediately regretting it.

She laughed, ‘Oh, I suppose you think you’re going to get rich and famous now you’ve been up there?’

I felt the joy drain. Exactly why I wished I hadn’t told Mum. Tracey was the same. They have this knack of just killing every possible joy with a sentence.

‘I don’t think so.’ I walked past and started to stock the counter trays. Counting the cakes as they went in. Spacing them exactly. Making sure I didn’t double tray anything in the same glass counter.

‘Ooo what’s got her goat?’ I heard it but chose to ignore and carry on as if nothing mattered. Nothing did matter. Not here anyway.

Betty came in as usual. I sat opposite her in Albie’s seat. ‘He’s busy today dear so you can sit there.’ Apparently, he was fixing some things for other people so couldn't make it for a cake, but she still took one for him. For later.

The days were the same and my week passed quickly. Busy in my mind and in my heart, I thought of Billy and the moment he had touched my face. The softness. The excitement of finding the bookshop on my own and of meeting Robert and his mother. I had to go again.

CHAPTER 41

Visiting self

It felt like I was asleep, but I couldn't be sure. I could see myself in bed. Head to the side and arms around the pillow tight. I was small and innocent. Unarmoured. I wanted to comfort her but there seemed to be a barrier between us. I tried to get closer to the bed, but it slid out of reach. Perplexed I sat down in the chair and watched me sleep.

As I started to relax more, the bat wafted in through the smallest of gaps in the almost closed sash window. It flapped wildly around my head. I swiftly covered my head and hair. Somewhere, a memory was triggered of a story from a long-gone grandparent. A time of the war when they were working for a family cleaning and they slept in the loft. Bats were aplenty and got tangled in one of the girls' hair. So, they always wore cotton bonnets to bed to avoid any further bat events. I didn't have a bonnet (not sure they made such things anymore anyway... a towel over the head would do!)

Still, I slept. I looked miniature. And I wondered who was caring for me. Who was keeping me safe? Was I safe? Yes, because I was watching over me.

A scent caught my attention. A warm rose with a topping of cut grass all collected. It's intensity beyond anything. There wasn't anything in my room that smelt that good. But... maybe... I hadn't noticed it.

The bat swung and flew, creating lines across the wall. Rolling thicker, wilder, and deeper. I could see the outline of what looked like a jagged entrance, a mound of rocks piled up but with an opening. A cave. Yes.

A figure appeared. Bob. Beckoning me to come with him. A hint of mischief in his eye and a daisy in one handheld out to me.

I felt a magnetic pull and stood. One eye on the tiny sleeping me and one on Bob. Could I bring her? Could I bring me? I mean little me.

He nodded vigorously. So much that I thought his head might fall off.

I walked towards the sleeping figure and met with a wall. Invisible. But not hard. Just a surface area that I couldn't get past. Bob held out his hand further with the daisy.

Why couldn't I get to me?

‘Darling Agnes, come with me. You have to come this way to get to you. We have to do a few giddy circles and you will come back on the other side and be with you,’ he gestured to the sleeping tiny figure. Besides, we are making a lot of noise. Aren’t we.....’

I smiled because I couldn’t speak or make a noise. Not in this space.

And so, I stepped forward. Bob took my arm and we descended down the steps, into the cave.

I held back as we got further in. It was damp and there was a trickle of water. The hairs all over my body stood out. Reaching for something but not the dank walls.

I stood in the dark wilderness with Bob at my side. He smiled boyishly at me and then revealed a large axe.

‘To the light Agnes. To... the ... light.’

With large lunges the wall started to shatter. Little poles of light shone through embracing and warming the cave. The unforgiving slams gradually cascaded the wall and let in light which fed all corners, holes and shelves. Opening up the hollowness and allowing the darkness to surrender to the light. I felt the warmth of sun smother my whole body; enveloping, holding, keeping safe.

'Agnes,' Bob whispered right into my ear.

I opened my eyes to see him looking closely at my face.

'It's time. Come on.' Grabbing my hand, he pulled me gently out of the cave and into a luscious landscape of white, purple, blue, green, yellow, orange and red. The beauty stilled me. If I could have stood there forever, I would have.

A waterfall stood moments ahead. Getting closer as we walked into the bright and brilliant colour of light. I bounced with every step. Revelling in the feeling of pure... just pure joy. Nearing the waterfall, I could see a small figure sat on a rock, their back to me. A beautiful floral dress framing them. I started to get a clearness of colour of hair, frame, movement. And then the understanding of connectedness.

The figure turned. A forlorn little girl. Mousey blonde hair, a look of anxiety, and limbs that would match a spider. Me. A smaller me.

'Agnes,' the low whisper gently caressed my ear. 'Meet Agnes.'

She turned and looked toward me as our name echoed across the space. I like to think there was hope in the look. My heart was pulled and stretched. Everything that surrounded us that was green became more vibrant, more prominent. Taking us all into this greenness.

The voice came from a different place not from Bob. Somewhere inside of my head. 'What do you need to tell her?'

The thought ricocheted. Until I moved forward. My movement seemed to still everything around. The fountain held its flow; the butterflies stopped mid flutter; Bob stood smiling with one hand on his hip and the other on his chest.

As I tentatively took step after step, starting to flow through the space as though on a travelator, a warm feeling wound around me that seemed to spill out from the green grass, trees, plants and moss. Pulsating warmth as I got closer and closer to my little, lovely, Agnes.

Her head hung low. I was unable to make eye contact this close. Unable to speak, I reached down and touched her hand, then held it. She allowed her hand to be lifted and stood in front of me. As her head slowly tilted, her eyes searching mine, I felt the most tremendous pull from my heart. An overflowing of joy, warmth and safety all wrapped into a ball. Love. I pulled her into me. Tight.

CHAPTER 42

Reaching others

I woke clutching the pillow. Feathers sticking out as if trying to escape. The alarm parping at me. 6.00am. It was time to move.

I felt invigorated and more energetic than I had in some time. Humming my way round the room as I dressed and checked how I looked in the mirror. Dancing and swaying in my dress, the cake dress, from side to side. Taking a look over one shoulder, then to the side. A wink here and there. *Yes, today is going to be a good day*!

The sun was out, and I smiled all the way to the bakery. I smiled at the grumpy looking lady at the bus stop – the corners of her mouth twitched as she suppressed a smile back. I smiled at the cars, the mums shouting at their kids, even the man raising his hands in frustration at the young boy on a scooter zipping in and out and around cars.

Turning the corner there were two people stood outside the bakery. They appeared to be having a conversation with Tracey who was stood in the doorway. She was tapping her watch and shooing them with her hand. I looked at my watch.

7.30am. I was late. They would normally be open now - maybe it was because I wasn't there. I moved quickly along.

As I entered Tracey was hot and her hair not in its usual precise place.

'Where have you been? I can't do all this setting up on my own and those bloody weirdos, with their ideas about spirits and angels and who knows what else mumbo jumbo, were trying to get in here. Give me strength.'

I decided to just agree. It wouldn't be helpful to make excuses or to say anything else. I popped my bag in the kitchen - no Ruth I noted - and returned to the front and finished off with the bread and cakes in the counter.

'Is Ruth ok?' I asked.

Tracey was still flushed.

'No, I can't do it on my own. She's ill or something. But she's never ill so I don't know what's going on there. Probably had a heart attack from all the cakes she eats. I told her yesterday that she needed to rethink her diet and she looked at me like she thought it was news. It's all over the papers about obesity and heart attacks. Doesn't she look in the mirror?'

I stood and looked at Tracey. Wondering if she had any idea what she had just said. If perhaps there was a way to tell her that this wasn't very kind. But I knew from her face that she wasn't going to hear me or even want to listen to what anybody else might think.

'I hope that you can pull your socks up with time keeping too young lady. There's plenty of others who want a job.'

'I'm sorry, it won't happen again.' I busied myself wiping down tables that hadn't been used, sorting things out in the kitchen that Ruth would normally do… and all the while I hummed. I knew it wasn't good to be late and I accepted that but there was no need to pull poor Ruth to shreds. I decided I wouldn't let it ruin my smiling. Right there and then I chose to smile all day… for Ruth.

People came in, in droves. It was the busiest day I'd had in the bakery. I didn't have to speak to Tracey. We were never alone until the end of the day. Everything sold.

I cleared and cleaned so that everything was spotless.

Tracey hovered around the counter. 'See you tomorrow Agnes…. On time.'

'Yep, see you.' I stepped out of the door without a look back. Headed left and towards Moon Street to drop in and see if Ruth was okay. I noticed that the rows of houses looked like faces. All connected. All looking the same. Open mouths and wide eyes. Some with one eye half blinking and others asleep.

Ruth lived just off Moon Street in a cul-de-sac. I wandered in looking for number thirty-three. It was right in the centre at the top of the keyhole. It was very clean looking and neat. Perfect almost.

The doorbell chimed out. Calling the dead, or half the street.

I stood waiting a little too long. To the point where I was about to press again. But the door opened. A large lady who highly resembled Ruth, with fearful looking eyes stood before me. She scanned me, and then returned to my face.

'Is...Ruth home?'

'Yes she is. Who are you?' The echoes of distrust curled around the words.

I smiled. 'I'm Agnes... from the bakery....I work with Ruth.'

'Oh.' The silence toe curling.

'Yes, I..err... was just seeing if she was ok?'

'Why wouldn't she be?'

I wondered whether to just turn and walk back up the path, out of the keyhole. But not this time.

'Agnes, what you doing here?' Ruth stood behind her mum. Or her mum stood in the way – I wasn't clear. I could see she looked like she had been crying but otherwise the same as always. There was a guarded look in her eyes and I wondered if her mum knew she was supposed to be at work.

'I was just thinking about you and thought I would pop by and say hi... just... you know. Oh and maybe if you wanted to go to the market. Would love to go on Friday if you fancy it?'

Her face lit up and I could see my Ruth in there, just for a moment. Her mum stood looking at me, like I was an extra-terrestrial and then turned to look at Ruth to see if she was possibly thinking of going out with this being from another place.

The look was enough to return Ruth to her original state. I continued to smile, to not get drawn into this familiar dynamic that I knew so deeply. I wanted to reach out and grab Ruth and pull her far, far away. But the presence of her mum was like a six-foot deep, solid wall.

'Ruth needs to rest now, don't you love.' Ruth nodded her head at such a speed I thought it would fall off.

The door was closed as I stood facing it.

A slight welling of tears came and went. I turned and headed back to Moon Street, past the bakery, and feeling released, I headed home.

CHAPTER 43

Living in joy

Friday, my favourite day and then off to London again tomorrow. The thoughts of all good things made me smile. I put on my brooch, feeling the slim petals and the emboldened central yellow area. Today was a yellow day I noted as I looked in the mirror. I hadn't consciously chosen what to wear. But it felt like a good colour for a Friday.

Mum was sat down staring at the television.

'You okay Mum?'

'Yes. Why wouldn't I be?' her questioning look made me wonder if she realised that the TV wasn't actually on. And maybe she did because she reached for the remote and blocked me from her thoughts as she delved into morning television.

'See you later.' No response.

Would she just sit there for the rest of her days? I didn't know for sure. But I did know there was a lot more going on out there. I breathed in the morning air and closed my eyes just for a moment revelling in the fact that I was here.

I wandered past the park on my way, the sun lit up the grassed open space. It looked like the grass had been cut. Edges were neat so all the paths seemed sharper. Clearer lines. Like a maze of pathways to choose from.

When I reached work the door was open. Ruth was in the back shuffling a cake into her mouth as I went in.

I jumped into the kitchen, 'Ha, caught ya.' We both laughed as she physically jumped and her mouth hung open a little until recognition dawned. She quickly closed her mouth and jawed the contents.

'You okay?' She nodded her head vigorously. I decided not to go further with what had happened the previous day. Maybe, just maybe, she wasn't ready to hear it yet… but one day.

'I thought we could go to the market and buy some jewellery.' She offered, cake-free.

'Yes, sure, I might see if they've got any nice dresses too.'

Ruth winked at me and beamed. 'Defo a dress. You look good in dresses.'

We were more misbehaved that Friday than ever before. I dropped a cake or two and even gave a few away for free to regulars who didn't seem to want to leave. We even sang. Which caused an avalanche of singing by some builders who daren't step into the bakery with their dusty boots on in case Tracey came along. Instead, they sang loudly until we gave them a doughnut each at the door.

'And don't come back again until next Friday Ruth taunted them!' I hadn't seen her so buoyant previously and even noticed the young builder hung back while the others wandered off.

'What's yer names?' he looked directly at Ruth. She looked at me uncertain. I urged her with my eyes. She blushed furiously and offered our names, while he coyly kicked the kerb and muttered something about popping by tomorrow.

Ruth's colour was intensely deep red. The urge to hug her was bypassed by her swift move to the kitchen where she stood peeking around the corner of the door. 'Has he gone?'

'Slowly Ruth, he's going slowly, I think he might be back to whisk you off your feet though.' That was too much, and she was gone into the toilet.

CHAPTER 44

New vision

The market was bustling. Vibrant and full of colour. I thought Ruth had bought enough jewellery to start her own stall, but my guess was it was as good as cake.

I tried on a green dress in the makeshift fitting room at the back of the tent covering the stall. Ruth stood guard while I undressed and reappeared.

When I stepped out, she looked like she might cry. 'Oh, does it look bad?' I felt my body start to cave a little, shrinking myself in case somebody saw. Ruth dragged me to the mirror.

'Oh my God Agnes, it looks beautiful. I mean you look beautiful. You could wear one of my necklaces with it.' She pulled a chunky one out and put it round my neck. 'Oh. No that doesn't work. They suit me not you.' We smiled at her directness.

'You do you,' I told her gently, 'and I'll do me'.

We walked back up the market and parted ways at the top. *Yes, I loved Ruth*. The thought rattled around in my head gently. And then it was gone. It was okay to love her I knew that. It felt right.

It was okay to love a lot of people. It didn't have to be one and not another. The thoughts filtered further. Even to the people I passed in the street.

I wasn't ready to go home so detoured into the park. Taking in the glorious colours and smells of nature. The smiles of some and the sadness of others. I followed a random path and enjoyed the warmth of the sun on my face and the idea that it was all okay.

As I came to Bob's bench and sat down, I wondered if Hagrid had been here today yet. Had I missed him? It had been over a week since I had come here. Then, onwards to tomorrow I hoped that I would see Billy again. And find the bookshop too. My thoughts dived this way, down and up. A maze of pathways on their own.

Whilst I was on this thought journey somebody sat down beside me. A flowery smell wafted under my nose. Pleasant but not overpowering. I looked from the corner of my eye. The clothes were worn and holes growing around the knees, less as a fashion statement more from oldness. The hems of the trousers broken revealing sock-less ankles, slightly swollen and marked. A little like Hagrid's - I thought - but they were clean.

A grunt nuzzled its way out of curls neatly framing the head and chin. I turned briefly, compelled to see the full picture. The look was complete with sunglasses masking his eyes and a coat that seemed its zip would never meet.

A plane flew over, causing distraction, and a look up to the clear blue sky. I pondered for a moment on where he had come from, and was going to, before shifting to my own journey for the coming days. Up early, so I could spend more time with the books, in the light. It felt so very different from here. Free. I breathed in deeply, drinking in the view all around me.

'What you thinking about?' The voice sounded oddly familiar. I turned towards the man, double checking what I had taken in before - the short curls, slightly ill-fitting clothes and flowery smell, all remained the same.

'I'm sorry?' I felt confused.

'Well, if you're looking up at the sky and down and then back up again you must be thinking of something.'

The body didn't match the voice. It was confusing.

'Yes, I understand but.... do I know you?'

He laughed. In a way that clarified some things but discounted others – I just didn't recognise him.

We remained in silence until he stood up and wandered slowly off, turning once. He waved.

I held up a hand. Bye... whoever you are.

The sun shone directly at me, dazzling, and telling me it was time to go back home. Maybe have a bath. Yes.

CHAPTER 45

Releasing patterns

The wind blew the curtains out, billowing into the room and sending hair clips, make up, clothes, ribbons to the floor. The bat flew in and hovered. Eyes wide open.

I sat up and watched. The light from the street pouring in and spot lighting the wall, the stage. There was no hanging around. The wall became a shower of light opening up into deep intense colours. I was quickly taken to the waterfall where she sat on the rock. The little me. This time she was facing out. Looking. Waiting. I walked towards her without hesitation and picked up her hands.

She looked up. Exploring my face. Her energy was different, mine too. There was no chatter just understanding, hearing despite the silence, although the rush of water played behind us.

Her hand in mine, a magnification, and a perfect fit, we stepped forward. Into the greenery of perfect grass and giant-leaved plants all wrapped around amazing buds of purple and pink.

I could hear voices. First ramblings, then fully formed words, succinct, and sharp. Bouncing around the space, off of rocks and trees. Keeping the little one close we wandered deeper into the woods. Exploring. Touching plants and flowers, trees, and watching the wild animals as they walked around us.

As we moved forward the voices started to get louder. Recognition. And a sense that we had been here before.

'Oh, she just doesn't know what she's doing from one minute to the next.' I heard the tones of my mother. Floating through. They were followed by, 'It's all in your heart Agnes, all in your heart.' Hagrid too. 'I think it was yours all along Agnes, the daisy suits you... it never belonged to anyone.'

'You're late, you're always late... and is that... alcohol I can smell on you young lady...People smell what they are.'

A cacophony continued. Buzzing around like gentle bees. I could hear but it didn't touch me. My little me looked up, a smile spreading. I held her close as we walked in the clearing amongst people who stood talking, smiling, spilling out light from their whole body it seemed.

It felt like I was sunbathing fully clothed. The warmth penetrating and surrounding my body. And a sense that I had stepped into a different world. The people here were all in their open space. Not so close as to touch nor so far as to have to shout. I began to feel like I would burst with a feeling of inner joy, excitement and pure, pure bliss. That feeling. True and unconditional love. Freedom.

And that was where we sat me and me embracing the feeling.

CHAPTER 46

Energy

I woke. Saturday, and sun pulsated through the window. Smiling to myself I danced my way through dressing, a little make up and a wink to myself.

The steps down the stairs revealed Mum's feet, legs then whole body, facing the TV. Her look told me she was unsure of what she was seeing. Was that fear?

'Where are you going?'

'I'm meeting a friend from work.'

'There's been lots on the news about stabbings and all sorts of strange people doing bad things so just keep an eye on what you're doing. People coming into the country on dinghies you just don't know what they're bringing in with them, all sorts of diseases. Just look....' she gestured towards the TV. I had switched off.

'See you later mum.'

I left her engrossed in her world of stabbings and disease-ridden immigrants and stepped out into the fresh air of mine.

As I walked past the park I thought of Hagrid. Was that actually him I had seen yesterday? An upgraded version. I laughed to myself at the possibility that it might have been. That he had bettered himself, stepped out of tramp-hood. Or maybe, just maybe, he never had been one. I wondered what he would be doing now. What would you do after being a tramp? I didn't see him being anything else. But then a tramp doesn't have to be an unwashed, smelly person, did they? Stopping to look in at the park it seemed brighter today, with the sun wakening and nurturing everything in there from the benches and trees, to the people; both young and older playing together.

My walk to the station took me past the bakery. I could smell the cakes, the sweetness loading in to the air as I got closer. Inside, Tracey was serving with her usual stony glare. Customers returned the favour. I tapped on the window and waved but chose not to wait for a response since I might have found myself turned into a rock on the side of the road too. I almost skipped the rest of the way.

The carriage was full today. Having to stand, I was between two teenagers and a man dressed in a suit. He was agitated and speaking loudly on his phone at a work colleague who was clearly not getting the opportunity to speak as there were no gaps. An endless string of condescension.

His arm pressed firmly against mine as he became unbalanced. I tried to move away but found myself moving into the teenagers who stood with their heads in phones. My 'excuse me,' resulted in blankness to my dilemma. I was wedged the whole journey between anger and disregard. It felt like I had taken the growing potion and just did not fit. Uncomfortable and irritated I started to wonder if it had been such a good idea at all. It wasn't starting well. What was to come? Maybe I wouldn't be able to find the shop on my own. What if Robert wasn't there? What if it didn't feel the same? What..... if....

I almost fell out of the carriage, it was so packed by the time we sailed into London's Charing Cross. I felt the tears coming, tapping the backs of my eyes. Hopelessness rattling around in my head like an overstaying old friend. I stood back until everybody had filtered through the barrier. Unsure whether I should go through it or turn and get back on the train. I waited until the train had filled with those leaving and had left the station. Only then did I feel the urge to move forward and go through the exit. Swiftly, easily, effortlessly I stepped into the station concourse.

Heading towards the exit I was met with a cordon and a bright yellow jacket.

'No exit this way luv…. You'll have to go out onto Villiers Street.' His arm extended towards another exit with steps descending. I took the steps and came out onto the street. Paved, with no cars and people spilling out of cafes and bars. I had been shrunk back down to further than normal size it seemed. I couldn't see any signs and the street continued endlessly in both directions.

Just ask someone. Ruth's best advice whispered. Choosing the right person was a different matter.

'Excuse me,' I reached out quietly to a woman passing who either didn't hear me or chose not to. And again with a young couple. I felt my heart drumming, letting me know that things weren't how I wanted them to be and perhaps I should just head back into the station and go home.

No. No. I wasn't going to. I hummed to myself, feeling the vibration in the back of my throat and into my head.

'You okay?' a young woman stood next to me. Dyed pink hair and a ring through her nose that I couldn't stop looking at. I wondered if it had hurt and why she wanted it.

'Hello...' she waved a hand in front of my face. 'I said did you need help, are you lost or something? Seen that expression before is all.'

I realised my whole body was tense and then relaxed as I did a half laugh. 'Sorry... I haven't got a clue where I am.'

'I am Ania by the way. Shall we start with where you're heading for first and then maybe I can help you find it?'

We sat and had a coffee. My first in London. And not my last with Ania it later transpired. She talked a lot about the time she had spent in London so far and how an artist had got her a job at the Central Drawing School. She loved to draw pictures of clowns. Of all the acts in the circus because, 'They are all the people that you meet – all of them depicted in the circus."

Ania nodded towards a woman walking by in incredibly high heels, taking slow deliberate steps, gently forward as if she were walking a tight rope. A kind of stilted walk. We both smiled at the illusion.

‘So, Agnes, where is it you’re heading to … that’s what we were going to sort.’

I fumbled in my handbag. Not quite sure what I was looking for, the business card I suppose. But I already knew it was Cecil Street.

‘You know what, I’m sure I know where it is. I’m okay. I was a bit disorientated coming out of the station but I feel like I’ll be okay.’

‘Cool, as long as you’re sure. I’ll be here for a while if you change your mind as I’m meeting a friend later now – we’re going to an exhibition. Hey if you want to join us, we’ll be meeting here at seven o’clock.’

‘I may do that.’ I smiled back at her and headed up Villiers Street all the way to the top. I found myself popping out next to the front of the station and straight into a bee hive. People moving this way and that. Cars, buses, bikes all moving swiftly. Every now and then car horns, setting off further car horns, as a blockage ceased movement. The cacophony continued and then released once the blockage freed and flow started again. The clock outside a shop read 11.11am in flashing neon numbers. I had plenty of time.

I found myself drawn along to Trafalgar Square where the morning sunshine lit up the area promoting its grandness. I felt the shrinking beginning again but continued to move up in the direction I had come from last time.

It felt like I moved easily. Effortlessly. A floating, travelator walk that didn't allow me to stop until I got to the end. The end stopped right at the alley way.

The alleyway seemed wider or maybe just lighter this time. The shops on one side radiated out their light in hues of yellow. Illuminating the doors and small windows opposite which seemed to echo back an orangey colour. I didn't hesitate. Stepping in I felt like I had been swathed in sunlight and warmth. Welcoming doorways slowed my journey as I lingered. Taking my senses on a waltz, I felt the kindness of each stranger as they beckoned me in.

At the end of the alley, illuminated by the experience, I stepped lightly across the road. The shop window had changed. A large orb sat in the middle radiating light all around the set. Twinkling, as it flashed in small sections.

The door was open, so without hesitation I stepped in. Surrounded again by the rays of golden light. Intense but warm. I squinted briefly but adjusted quickly.

'Ah Agnes, you're here. I've been expecting you.' Robert stood by the door and tipped his head in a bow.

'I'm so glad to be here, it's been quite a journey this morning.' I exhaled in a ball of agitated excitement.

'Trains, darling Agnes. All that energy fizzling into you.'

'There was a really grumpy man, and I was sandwiched between him, the doors and a couple of teenagers. None of them gave me any space.'

'Oh, crumpling your wonderful energy Agnes, we can't have that.' Robert wafted his arms around my head. I stood rigid.

'All done.'

'Was it a fly?'

'Ha, no Agnes dear, not a fly.'

'Robert!' the voice from above. His mother was in again.

He smiled politely, 'I'll be right back.' He mounted the stairs in large lunges, effortlessly.

Something was different this time. The colour sizzled out from the shelves. The light rained down through the very large windows. Above, I could see that open windows were dotted in the ceiling, beaming further light down in square patches. A berry landed near my feet. I squinted up to see where it might have come from. Looking further around the floor I could see other similar splats of varying colours.

'Why would you leave them open?' I muttered allowed.

'Because we need to have a top up from nature.' Robert stood looking matter of fact.

'Oh,' was all I could offer.

I was ushered to the upper floor. It was clear. The window was open. As I mounted each step the view became clearer until I stood firmly on the wood flooring looking out across to the horizon. Across London. Across the highs and the lows of the architecture running for miles and creating patterns knitted together by roads.

'Isn't it beautiful,' he whispered into my ear.

At that moment a light seemed to speed across the sky in the distance. Faint, but there. We exchanged a look and returned our viewing.

‘A shooting star Agnes. It’s a celebration.’

‘In the daytime? Don’t they happen at night-time?’ I quizzed.

‘Of course, but if you’re very lucky and unblocked you’ll see them in the daytime too. Not many have this view, Agnes. Drink it in.’

He left me stood there. Books framing the view. All else was just bright daylight consuming the space. I wondered what it would look like at night. On a clear night. Or an unblocked one… was that what he meant?

I went close to the window so I couldn’t see the books. Overcome by the sensation that I was flying, I allowed myself to scan the miles to the horizon.

‘What you doing?’ the little old lady stood right behind me, hands on her hips.

I pointed feebly at the window. ‘Just looking at the view….,’ she continued to frown and stare deeply into my eyes so much that I felt the need to explain further, ‘It is beautiful so I just wanted to look closer. And it makes you feel like you’re flying. Have you seen it…?’

'Of course I've seen it,' she smiled revealing a set of very good teeth. They held my gaze. How was that possible? 'But it's better if you come up higher.' She headed towards the ladder.

'Oh no,' I stepped forward as if I were going to stop her. Soon realising that it was a pointless effort. 'You shouldn't do that without .... '

'Without what? I'm not that old dear. Last time I checked I was 25. Don't ever look in the mirror dear, it does tell little fibs sometimes. And we all need a little bit of fun. Besides, you're here, so you can supervise.' She smiled exposing her set of amazingly straight, white teeth. Again, I was transfixed.

I let her lead. The ladder had wheels at the bottom and was on a rail fixed to the top shelf. Her agility matched mine and yet I could see the creped skin and blood bruises of a person who had spent some time alive. She stepped up until there were just two steps remaining, me on the rung two below this and with just a view of books. This particular row was all numbered. 111, 222, 333. I reached out to touch.

'What are you doing?' her sharpness had my hand move at the speed of light back to the ladder. She looked down where my hand had been. 'No touching, not yet anyway. We haven't finished this bit yet.' Her playfulness was illuminated by another wide smile.

'I'm going to sit up here so you can climb higher. Or you can go down and take the brakes off. Now that would be fun,' she nodded her head and ushered me down to do as I was told.

I looked over the balcony quickly. Wondering if I should call Robert even with the prospect of getting into trouble with... Mum. He was leaning half under a curtain in the front window. All I could see were legs.

'Come on, stop dilly dallying.' This had me back over to the ladder and releasing the brakes. 'Right, I've got hold of it up here. Up you come.' As I looked up she had transferred herself to a sitting position, now with her back to the view. I marvelled at her seeming ability to move so swiftly. How was that possible? Was it possible? A little old lady?

You are going mad Agnes, this can't be real.

But still I climbed the ladder tentatively in case it moved quickly. As I got closer to the top and towards her, I started to see the view. The colours. The patchwork effect magnified. Light upon light shining down and illuminating the movement of tiny people; an ant farm. Lines running up and down. Across. Some going around in circles. The grey buildings were replaced by yellow sandy colours, purples and a sort of blue tinge. The sun reflected off windows creating dazzling sparkle.

'You know what… Agnes… is that your name?' I nodded, 'Agnes, I have been here a very long time and I have looked out at this view every day and it never changes. It is so magic and it never fails to move me to a tear.' She wiped underneath her eye dramatically.

'It looks a little different from down there though I think,' I pointed out.

'No Agnes, it doesn't look any different dear not at all. It is the same,' she responded knowingly.

'But I don't think it looks as ….. grand…. From down there.' I was keen to get my point across.

'Yes, dear, it looks the same whether the sun is shining on it or there is torrential rain.'

A rising within me signalled my irritation at the fact that it obviously looked different when it was sunny to when it was raining.

'You see, my dear, the way that you are. Whatever you are feeling in here,' she tapped at the middle of her chest, 'You will see out there.'

It was a moment where something released in my mind. There was a recognition of this. An understanding.

'So if I'm feeling sad then I will see sadness?' I offered, not quite sure this was possible.

'Well almost that yes. But how do you see the world when you are feeling sad?'

'I think I just get really negative and everything seems black and white and not very nice and nothing goes right.'

'That's it my dear. But the most exciting bit is when you sit in the most exciting feeling of the most exciting thoughts of the most exciting dreams... then you will see this.'

She waved her arm out at the view and showed me those amazing set of teeth again.

It was then that I remembered what Hagrid had said, 'People smell how they are'. Yes. 'People smell how they are,' I muttered. I beamed as the revelation of understanding consumed me.

‘I do not smell young lady!’

‘Oh no, no I…’

‘No time for that let’s go for a ride.’

The next thing I knew I was zipping along the shelves, clinging on with a pair of crepe skinned legs right in front of me. Joining in with the ‘weeeee’ as we zipped along one way and then the next. This was how I felt.

‘What on earth?’ Robert’s whispery boom filled the balcony. ‘Mother, you are teaching lovely Agnes some very fine things, but I do think it’s time for your rest. You have been told about overexerting yourself.’

Robert stopped the ladder and assisted both of us down.

‘It’s time, mother, to rest those legs.’ I watched them walk. Robert holding her arm gently, taking slow graceful steps. Whilst his mum shuffled appropriately beside him.

CHAPTER 47

We are one

I sat at the desk waiting. Wondering how they were able to keep the shop going as nobody seemed to come in. Not while I was there anyway. I looked at my watch. Six hours had passed.

'Oh, she really is a one, Agnes,' he smiled the same smile as hers. The same teeth.

'I think she rather likes you.'

'She does?' I waited, looking, wondering why.

'You think that perhaps she wouldn't?'

'Well... I don't know.... I... she didn't really seem either way.'

Robert fumbled underneath the table, in a drawer. Looking up at me above the table and then down at where he seemed to be rifling... throwing odd bits from the drawer. Paper, paper clips, pens. And then a daisy on a keyring.

He held it out to me. A long arm with a dainty daisy at the end.

Mouth agape I took it. Fingering the petals and the centre piece. Yes. It felt exactly the same. I ruffled through my handbag pulling out hankies, receipts, pennies. In the side section lay the daisy brooch that Billy had given me. I held it out next to the keyring. Like one of those hearts broken in two finding its other half but instead two whole daisies. Full of life, new beginnings, and a connection with each other.

Neither of us spoke. Robert tilted his head to one side and winked. I …. well, I just smiled the biggest smile with the biggest teeth.

CHAPTER 48

Bathed in light

Robert stood at the door. 'I'm with you always my darling Agnes.' He touched his heart.

I felt tears. For an ending. But somewhere within me I knew it wasn't. It would never end.

Breathing in the sun, the air, and the idea that I could see things as I felt. I let it all envelop and then flow through. Stepping down from the doorway I looked back into the shop window.

Books were placed all around. Different colours, genres, titles. A hand reached in and placed a crystal ball at the centre of the books. At that moment everything reflected. I could see the titles, colours, pictures and more returned to their source. A vibration rebounding back creating a spectacular scene.

I laughed aloud in the air. As I knew, finally, I knew how it worked. It all started within me.

A couple walked by engaged deep in conversation, touching hands, and laughing. Then more people until it was densely populated like an incoming ant crew. Some stopping at the book shop, mesmerised by the front window. Others enjoying the sun and talking randomly to different people.

Back across the road was the alley which was now full of exuberance and spilling out the traffic of shoppers on a continuous conveyor belt.

I decided to go down Cecil Street. Taking a different route. Feeling the warmth and pull of something new. The street widened as I walked down. Shops became larger and then taller, exquisite buildings that had seen the comings and goings of seasons both in weather and in life's cycles. Their years of knowledge and experience beating loudly into the street.

At the end of Cecil Street there was a sign. Old, with all its original features, it gave a choice; to the left was 'Theatre Land' and to the right 'Oxford Circus.'

To the circus it is Agnes.

CHAPTER 49

Sharing the gift

My afternoon was spent laying in the park soaking up the sun. Watching the passing cars and people. Some extravagant, some less so. I wondered where they were going. What they were thinking. If they were happy, sad, or just going along with life.

I propped myself up on my elbows and picked daisies. Digging a hole in the stem of one to interlace the next through. Creating a circle. Then over my head to wear as a necklace. I admired it, touching the daisies gently.

As I wandered, people stopped me and admired the necklace. 'How beautiful,' and 'Oh gosh, I think I'm going to have to make one,' and 'That looks lovely on you.'

An empty bench offered a nice place to sit. A plaque on the top wood slat caught the sun. 'For all those stars out there who have yet to find their shine – rest a while.' A reminder of Bob's bench in Purbrey Park, I sat and closed my eyes and visualised the park at home. The many paths and trees, and those moments with Hagrid and Billy. An all-encompassing feeling of warmth and happiness spilled over from inside and outside.

This was coupled with a scent. A delicate perfume. As I opened my eyes, a young woman was sat next to me. Her body hunched, hands clenched tightly. She looked down into her lap. Her shoulders moved a little as she sobbed, silently. The odd tear dropping down onto her hands.

I watched for a moment, the memories flooding back. Darkness, railway stations, drunken days and nights morphing. They came, flowed through and went as the sun melted them away on their journey.

'Excuse me….,' I offered quietly. 'Are you okay?'

The young woman looked up towards me. Pale, tired and thin. I recognised this. I felt her pain flowing out and around her body. She remained silent. Unable to comprehend so unable to share. I reached out my hand and touched her arm gently.

'I'm Agnes.'

Acknowledgements

There are a few people who were monumental in bringing this story to life. In particular, Karen Stanley, (through her Write of Passage Growth Academy) who is the most amazing author, leader, mentor and publisher. Also, Bev Bunn, Jane Carson & Fiona Shoults, who are members of the Academy and were with me for the full journey.

Thanks also to those who have guided me over the years on my own journey. Tanja Jaeger (Tanja's Angels) who has taught me all I know so far about energy, angels and the spiritual world. Jackie Honsig-Erlenburg for being my closest ally in finding my own way in the light and, to my true self. Karen Spinks for riding the waves with me my whole life and always walking with me without judgement.

My gracious thanks to my family for just being there and accepting me for who I am in dark and light times. And for all of those who have inspired, lifted, guided, and loved me for me..... you know who you are.

Of course, there is, without doubt, a gratitude beyond words for Bob. Without him in my life, 'I Am Agnes', would never have been written at all.

Love and light x

About the Author

Jackie lives in London. She is the Founder of Move Your Mood UK and is a Movement & Energy Coach part-time and also works as an Administrator at King's College London. Passionate about mental health and energy work, she uses movement and holistic practices to help women find balance in their mood and energy.

She loves angels and all things spiritual.

Favourite quote: Nothing is ever quite as it seems – look again.

If you are affected by the events around mental health, and suicide references, in the earlier part of the book, please know that there are some wonderful organisations out there who may be able to help you. But sharing with somebody that you know can be the first step.

Printed in Great Britain
by Amazon

74933240R00163